Sunrise

at

7:12

Books *by* Alex B. Stone

Sunrise at 7:12
Country Boy
Shades of Benny Roone
Tales from the Prayer House
Benny Roone Detects
Summer
If I Could Sleep
Going Home
A Sabbath Walk

Sunrise

at

7:12

a novel

Alex B. Stone

Postern Press

SUNRISE AT 7:12. Copyright © 2014 by Alex B. Stone. All rights reserved. No part of this book may be reproduced, transmitted or stored by any means without written permission except in the case of brief quotations embodied in critical articles or reviews. For information, address Postern Press, P.O. Box 26228, Baltimore, MD 21210.

Printed in the United States of America.

This book is a work of fiction. The places, events and characters described herein are imaginary and are not intended to refer to actual places, institutions, or persons.

Library of Congress Cataloging-in-Publication Data
Stone, Alex B.
Sunrise at 7:12 / Alex B. Stone

First Edition: February 2014

To the memory of Martha

And to Anne, Clayton and Elizabeth

Book I

Chapter 1

Emma

Edith and Erna sleep until nine, come in, drink a glass of orange juice, and have the strength to go out and play tennis for an hour. For me, I have to prepare, plan for that nine a.m. tennis match: up at seven, do my stretches, have breakfast. By seven Mama has made coffee. Mama is on the porch in a yellow short-sleeved sweat suit, coffee cup in hands. She stands facing the Gulf. She waits for sunrise at seven-twelve. "Each morning it's different. You sleep well, Emmie?"

"The new mattress is a little too stiff."

"I'll get a foam pad for you."

"You don't have to, Mama."

"No problem, Emmie. You might just as well be comfortable."

In the predawn light Papa does his back exercises, twenty modified situps, five knee to chest, right knee, left knee. Papa puts his pillow on the porch table, eases his chest onto the pillow, does ten up and back leg lifts, then ten deep knee bends, followed by ten leg on the table stretches held to the count of twenty.

"Glad you got up, Emmie."

"A russet sun this morning."

"Yesterday the sun was rising in the east, the moon was setting in the west."

Mom and Dad leave for their walk to the Hilton, return with *The New York Times*. For me, breakfast is grapefruit quarters, Grapenuts, and skim milk. Mom has put out bagels, cream cheese, lox, and muffins: bran, corn, blueberry.

"You ought to eat more, Emmie."

"I'm not going to look like Edith. All she has to do is quit eating, then she wouldn't have to hide herself under that black coverup."

"Emmie, let's go shopping. I don't like it when it gets busy at Jerry's Market."

Mama shops with coupons: coffee, yogurt, pizza, a dollar off here, fifty cents there. The total credit is $3.40. Add the value of the soap, skin lotion, shampoo, and conditioner Mama collects from the Marriott hotels on the trip down, Mom no doubt saves $4.00 a week from her grocery bill. I have heard it from Dad since . . . since forever. "A penny saved is a penny earned."

"It's the immigrants who adapted Benjamin Franklin's WASP frugality."

"Not all the immigrants, Papa. Look at Bernie's folks, a house in London, spring vacations in Tuscany."

"That's second generation immigrant, Emma, not first."

So Papa reminds us all the time, "A penny saved is a penny earned."

And then what? Then Papa gives it away to me, to Edith, to Erna, to his college, to this and that. Papa has no fear of tomorrow, not for him, the tomorrow of nursing homes and wheelchairs. No fear that he won't have enough for his "old age." That's his religious faith, faith in the Lord our God; so he thanks God and pursues lawsuits. (Pursue justice and mercy, Perform deeds of loving kindness.) "We have to, Emma, because we can afford to. If we won't, who will?" Erna can't help. Edith does all she can. Me? My Ph.D. in Urban Studies is no asset to running Kramer Companies.

"What should I do with money you give me, Papa?"

"Spend it, Emma. If there is something you and Bernie need, spend it, but if you don't need it—"

There it is, the disclaimer to spending and the advisory to save.

"Save for what, for when?"

"For when you may need it."

That's the extent of the financial advice received from my father. I didn't learn much more from Dad when I would come downtown to Kramer Companies. That was when I was home from college and came downtown to his fifth floor office.

"Your office looks like something out of Dickens. Liven it up, Papa."

"Do what you like, Emmie."

I did. Today his two-room suite is refurnished in contemporary Scandinavian, with two red upholstered Herman Miller desk chairs for Mom and Dad, and four pseudo-Breuer side chairs for the occasional insurance salesman. I, too, have joined with Edith and Erna. "Papa, try, try to get out more, get rid of your day to day responsibilities. You don't need the money."

"It's not the money, Emmie. Who else will do it."

"Just quit, Papa."

"Only the employed can do that. The self-employed don't have those options. You, you have tenure, you get a pension. In time you take your personal papers out of your desk. You are retired. You take up the cello, you become a consultant. You travel to South Africa on a grant. The poor tax payer, he pays for all that. Higher real estate taxes or higher income taxes pays your salary, provides for your health care, pays your pension. Someone does all that for you. For the self-employed, we do all that ourselves. No wonder I don't do it well. I have to be an expert in buying life insurance, property insurance, tax shelters. Forget it, Emmie. I got no choice. As my Uncle Al used to say, 'In is easy, out is hard.' "

"Papa, it's not a joke."

"All right, Emmie, it's not a joke. So?"

"So, try, Papa. It's for your own good. Travel, take a cruise, go to the Caribbean."

"Mama gets seasick."

"Papa."

"Emmie, don't worry. I'll tell you a story. A story my mother told me."

That's my dad with what begins as a simple conversation becomes a story, a moral fable, or a lecture.

"The good Lord said, 'Now, Al, all your life you have been a good and kind and generous man. You have prayed to me for help with your burdens. Al, I will help you. Bring me a sack. I will put all your troubles in your sack. Then you will take your sack to the town square. You will find other sacks there. I can't take away your burdens, your responsibilities, because those are your life, but I can exchange them for you. Al, you may exchange your pack for any in the town square. Next Friday morning go to the town square to exchange your troubles and sorrows. Be not fearful. Be not hasty, choose carefully.' "

"So?"

"Al brought his sack to the piles of sacks. Being a wise man, Al tried each and every sack in the pile. He lifted them, he tossed them over his shoulder. He carried them on his shoulder. He lifted them with one hand, with both hands. At noon, Al stopped to eat his frugal lunch, a piece of black bread, a head of garlic, and an apple. He shut his eyes to rest. It was then he heard God again. 'You must reach a decision by an hour before sunset, for it is against the law to carry on the Sabbath.'

"Al went through the sacks again, arranged them into piles, rearranged them, then he chose. And when he got home and opened the sack, he found that he had chosen his very own sack, because for him his own burdens were the easiest to bear."

"Papa, did your mother really tell you that? It sounds like an old wives tale to me."

"I thought it was one of Mama's Yiddish stories, but one day I walked into the chapel at Stanford University. You want to hear the story of my revelation, Emmie?"

"Not now, Papa, later."

"In the chapel this very story is engraved on the granite walls. Of course, it's told better than I did."

"You wouldn't lie to your daughter, would you, Papa?"

"No, Emma, not knowingly."

I went over, kissed Papa on his forehead. "I'll have to remember that story."

"Forget it and you can drive to Palo Alto, see for yourself."

"I will, Papa." I laughed.

"Don't you trust me?"

"Not a matter of trust. It's a matter of confirmation."

"Emmie, if you don't get nominated or don't get elected, promise me something."

"What, Papa?"

"Don't get discouraged, that is, for any length of time. Whatever will happen, it will be for the best. *Gom zo le tova*. This too is for the best."

"With that philosophy, Papa, our world may not get much improvement."

"It doesn't mean that at all, Emmie. It simply means

don't get discouraged, channel your efforts in another direction, but keep trying. 'It's all for the best' is a Hebrew survival mantra."

"Papa."

"Yes."

"Nothing . . . What was it like in the prison camp?"

"I survived."

"You didn't say this too was for the best."

"I learned a lot."

"What did you learn, Papa?"

"What we all learn, Emmie. We live alone, we die alone. What makes survival possible is hope and having somebody you can count on. That is when you need support, when you can no longer carry on." Dad stopped. Then, "I was lucky I had Duane Gustafson."

"Who?"

"Duane Gustafson. The Dane, I called him. He looked out for me. Duane made me eat, made me take care of myself; you ask Mama about Duane."

"I never heard Mama talk about him."

"Duane is dead, went back to that little town south of Des Moines, worked himself to death, trying to catch up all those years he lost."

"What did he do?"

"He became a veterinarian, a country doctor. Up and down the roads, up at dawn, didn't quit until he saved the life of every cow in the county, worked days and nights."

"What happened?"

"Margaret, Duane's wife, called me. 'Bob, Duane is dead.' It was about ten years ago. So we went to the funeral. There was The Dane in an open coffin. Duane looked twenty years older than me, and he was two years younger. I guess developing housing is less killing than being a country vet, but you know what I think?"

"What, Papa?"

"Being a vet is more important."
"You done a lot of good, Papa."
"Not enough, Emmie, not enough. So, what will you do if you aren't nominated?"
"I'll have a baby, and in two years I'll try again."
"The best of all possible worlds."
"Is that Voltaire?"
"It could be."
"Mama would like that."
"Like what?"
"A grandchild."
"Wouldn't you?"
"Of course."
"Why don't you say so?"
"I don't like to order."
"I'm only thirty-six, Papa, don't worry, plenty of time."
"Your Mama was twenty-one when Edith was born. I was in the army, didn't see Edith until she was four months old. Mama never complained. Two children, two wars. We were almost afraid to have another child. Every time Mama got pregnant, there was a war."
"Papa, what was the war like?"
"Wars are about killing and getting killed."
The New York Times was on Papa's writing table. "Congress Votes War."
"Papa, will there be a war?"
"All the makings are ready. The reserves are being called up. I'll tell you a story."
"Papa, I am playing tennis at nine."
"Take it easy on Edith. She has an arthritic knee, the family weak link."
"Erna and Edith against me."
"That's only fair. You have more trophies. Emmie, you had better come and get your trophies. Mama is threatening to throw them out."

"Mama wouldn't do that."

"Well, it's one way to get you to come to Rock City."

"Bernie and I are hoping to get home for the Seder."

"It's early this year, end of March."

"I think we have a semester break then, and if not, Papa, we'll come home for at least the weekend."

"I would like to take Bernie out to the tree farm. He has never been on the farm.

"I'll tell him, Papa."

"Tell him to bring hiking boots. What time is it?"

"Papa, it's only eight-thirty."

"I thought it was later."

Erna came in. "Edith up yet?"

"Go wake her."

"Not me, I'm hungry."

It's Mama who goes into the guest bedroom to get Edith.

"Papa, O.K., make it short."

"Emmie, do you know you are the only one of my daughters who wants to hear my stories."

"Edith and Erna are waiting until they are published."

"No one wants my stories. I have given up on stories. Temporarily, of course."

"What are you writing?"

"A play about three daughters."

"I promise to read that."

"You'll see it on Broadway."

"Papa, you were telling me about the war."

"When our reserve unit was activated, we were assigned to Fort Riley in Junction City, Kansas. Most of us were twenty, twenty-one, and then there was a call up of reserve officers, captains, majors. They reported in World War I uniforms, in cavalry twills with yellow stripes and in boots with spurs. We had already been mechanized into infantry, infantry with two crossed sabers, cavalry collar emblems. Those officers were in their forties, and to us they looked like our fathers. We were pretty cruel to them, called them 'Pappy.' "

"So, Papa?"

"So it's all in perception. When I was twenty-one, forty-six was very old. Now Edith is forty-six, and to me she is still very young."

"Papa, I love you."

"Tell Mama."

"Tell her what, Papa? Can't you finish a sentence."

"Tell her you love her."

Edith came in, and it brought back thoughts of Edith and tennis and when we were all at home. Edith wouldn't let me keep score. Edith is like that; she likes to win, and if she can't win, well then, she won't score. Erna doesn't care. With her speed and the coaching she received, she could have been the number one singles player in the state. Erna took the easy way. She played doubles and became the runner-up at the state finals. Erna was never much for training. Getting up early, the jogging, that was not her thing. Erna would jog only after practice. One mile, no more. No matter what her coach, Mrs. Morgan, said. Erna got away with that because in high school she was number one without trying. When Erna got to State, she was sure she would do just as well there. The competition in Champaign was tougher, so Erna settled for the number four. Mama never asked. Papa never said, "You can do better." I guess I was the only one that was disappointed. When I think of what Erna could have been . . . Edith tried hard, but Edith . . . I don't know. Edith has all the strokes. Edith just has never developed court sense, always just a little too late. Now, Papa had it all, all the strokes, speed, court sense, timing, until he hurt his knees. Then his spine went out. There isn't one picture of Papa playing tennis, not one clipping from the sports pages. I saw them when I was six or seven, and then every memento disappeared from our family album that Mama keeps. Mama told me, "Papa threw all his clippings out. If Papa can't play, he doesn't want to remember when he did."

We were walking back from the court. It's across the road about four hundred feet from the cottages. Edith was wiping her face into a towel.

"I can't stop sweating. I have to start on a diet."

"Not here you don't. Mama won't allow it."

"I have to sit down." We sat poolside, Edith in the shade. Erna drank at the water cooler.

"Sit down, Erna, I'll only be a second. Wait for me. I don't want Mama to see me all tuckered out."

"You feeling all right?"

"I have been going through some tests."

"What for?"

"Nothing that is nothing life-threatening."

"O.K., tell."

"You won't tell Mama or Dad."

"You know me better than that."

"I had . . . I thought I had the flu. It turned out to be a viral pneumonia, and now I have pleural adhesions. Exercise is the best answer."

"You feel all right?"

"Better."

It was when we were eating breakfast. Now I am sure that Erna is sorry for what she said to Papa. She said it to Papa and Mama did not say anything, not a word. I saw my mom and dad look away, afraid to confront Erna. *Erna, that is no way to talk to us.* It's my fault, too. I should have said to Erna, "That is no way to talk to Mama and Papa." I hadn't said it then, in front of Mama and Papa. I should have later, when I was alone with Erna, showering. That's a family for you. The last couple of years Edith won't say anything more to Erna. Edith has given up on her. "It's

Erna's problem, her life. Always angry. Why should she be so angry with Mama and Papa? What could they have done that thirty-five years later Erna has to flare out at them?" It happened during breakfast. Who knows how things like that begin? Papa was reading *The New York Times* financial section. He read out loud something about a large developer from Indianapolis, Indiana, having lost almost everything, his racehorses, his limousines, his condo in New York, all because his projects didn't rent up quickly enough to provide the cash to pay his mortgage loans, so the banks were taking all his worldly assets. Papa said, "Now, Erna, when you open your gallery, don't spend it all, put aside about fifteen percent as a reserve." Mama was listening; she added, "You listen to Papa." Mama was smiling. That was sort of a dig at Papa's status as advisor, pundit to his daughters because not once in twenty years has one of his daughters consulted Papa about anything, financial, matrimonial, or international. Erna took it as Papa giving her instruction. "Papa, don't tell me how to run my life. You keep out of my business." And then she said, "You keep the fuck out of my life."

Mama didn't answer, stood up, went into the bathroom. Papa heard. He went back to reading. Edith made believe she hadn't heard, and I didn't say anything. I should have said Erna, "Look at what you did to Mama. Mama was crying. Papa got up, went in to Mama. I saw him kissing her shoulder, whispering in her ear. You made Papa apologize for you to Mama, something you should have done, not Papa. He was saying, 'Erna is sorry—she just doesn't know how to apologize. Erna is angry with me. It's nothing with you, Millie. She is angry at me because of Michael. So I say something and she strikes out at me.' "

"Erna shouldn't talk to you like that."

Papa said, "Erna shouldn't talk to anyone like that. It's a different generation, Millie, with a different language."

Erna never apologized. Papa took Mama out for lunch. For the rest of Erna's stay, Mama didn't talk to Erna.

By next year Erna won't be so angry, and if she still is, I'll take her aside and tell her, "You may not have noticed, but when you talk to Papa that way you cut him down. That's a deeply painful thing you did to Papa. The folks keep forgiving you, Erna. They never say anything, but not speaking to Mama and Papa that way is better. There is no need to be cruel."

"Emmie, I don't want Dad telling me what to do. I am a big girl. I can't stand being told what to do."

"Go back to your shrink, Erna, and let him teach you to be more forbearing, more forgiving to your parents. You know how much they care for you."

"They were too busy to care, Erna. They cared for their business."

"Don't dwell on the past, Erna. We have so little time left together as a family. Mama and Papa are getting older."

"You are the lucky one, Emmie, full of all that kindness and understanding, all that wisdom." That is how Erna always answered. So I didn't say anything. I just figured this outburst was like all the other incidents with Erna. Come Passover, Erna would get off the airplane in Rock City, and Papa and Mama would kiss her and no one would mention what was, and we would be a family again for a weekend or the few days we were together or until Erna blew it again.

Chapter 2

Emma

I don't know why Erna had to orchestrate her funding for the art gallery in Paris. I had tried to tell her, "Just tell Papa and Mama how it is."

"I have a complete business plan, Emmie."

That's the problem with Erna and Edith, all that business school education. They know all the reasons business fails. I had to listen to Erna's. "To succeed I need adequate capital. The reason that most business fails is insufficient capital."

"You worry too much, Erna. Papa doesn't give a damn about business plans. Papa will talk to Mama, he'll chuckle, and you will have your money."

"I have to be sure, Emmie. If Mama sells the cottages I'm sure there is enough."

"Erna, call Papa, tell him, prepare him."

Instead Erna calls Leroy Carlson, sics Carlson on Mama again. Mama is always polite to callers, that is, until you get into personal questions, so that didn't work. Mama wouldn't talk to Carlson until Erna came to Florida. Then of course she wouldn't say "No, Mr. Carlson," or "Too busy, Mr. Carlson," or "Not today, Mr. Carlson," because Mama didn't want to hurt Erna. She should have told Erna,

"It's none of your business whether I sell the cottages. You need, you are welcome to come to us. That's what parents are for, to help their children." I could see Mama's face when Carlson sat there facing her. Mama holding it all in, successfully, too. Mama didn't say a thing. Papa saw it too, and Papa kept quiet, all to save Erna's face in front of Carlson. Erna got her art gallery. I got support to run for Congress. Edith didn't want anything. I know Papa and Mama. When they send a check to Erna and me, they will send to Edith.

It's easier for me to talk to Papa when we are alone, just he and I around the dining room table. "Tomorrow you go back to 'educating the masses,' " is how Papa describes our remedial English department.

"Most of my students are in their late twenties. This is their last chance for an education."

"If not for the army, I wouldn't have had a chance."

Mama heard that. "Robert, that isn't so. You were working your way through college." Mama hears even if she is in the kitchen.

"The army made it easier."

Edith left on Monday, Erna on Thursday. Friday night it was just the three of us. Mama said the prayers for lighting the Sabbath candles, Papa the blessing over the wine and the challah.

I was a little girl again, going to services at the Rock City Jewish Center, sitting to the left of Papa, Edith and Erna between Papa and Mama. After dinner I was telling Papa, "Papa, I have students in the reserves; they are afraid of being called up."

"In every generation there are those who arise to destroy us. With God's help, they will be destroyed. Hussein is a tyrant who must be destroyed."

"Papa, how can you talk about God and war? In war

each side prays that their God destroy their enemy. God on both sides? What kind of God can that be?"

"You are right, Emmie, but tyrants have to be stopped."

"So Hussein has to be stopped, and men will die and women and children will die."

"It's a horror, Emmie. You are right. It's all a horror. I just don't know what the alternatives are."

"Kill. Kill. That's no answer."

"Since Cain and Abel. It's a just war."

"Was Korea a just war? Look what it did to you and Mama, look at the welts on your back." Papa only removes his T-shirt to go swimming. Then he pulls his trunks up to cover the scars on his left hip.

Papa didn't answer. He rose from the table, began to clear the dishes, then back to his armchair on the porch. Mama stacked. I tried to help. Mama wouldn't let me. "Emma, go sit with Papa on the porch. It will be very hard for him tomorrow, not to have you around."

Papa sits facing the full moon that has risen above the resident crow's palm tree. By their flashlights I make out walkers on the moonlit beach. The surf sounds rise with the incoming tide. Papa sits, turns towards me. "Sit down, Emmie."

"You O.K., Papa?"

"Just thinking."

"About what?"

"About things I hadn't thought about in forty years. About Korea. We thought it was a just war. We were the World War II generation. We had cleaned out Hitler and Mussolini and Tojo, and now we would bring justice and equal opportunity to all the Koreans."

"Nothing wrong with that, Papa."

"Tell that to the North Koreans. To them we were killers of women and children who had come thousands of miles to destroy their revolution."

"They told you that?"

"Each and every day. In a prison camp you can't not hear that."

"Did you believe that?"

"Killing women and children—that part. Bombs, artillery shells don't know women and children. One thing is for sure, we didn't bring democracy to Korea."

"That's not your fault, Papa."

"That's the trouble, Emmie, whom do you blame? Whose fault is it?"

Mama comes in with a tray of fruit, apples, grapes, strawberries, and a pear. Papa cuts the bell off the pear, gives it to Mama, cuts a side off, hands it to me, cuts the other side for himself.

"My mama, Emmie, when we were little, would peel an apple for us, then cut the first slice for herself before we got ours."

"Your mother wanted to be sure it was fit for her only son to eat." That from Mama.

"Too bad you never met my mama, Emmie. It wasn't easy for my folks. It's not easy for immigrants."

"Some of my Oriental students are doing very well."

"It's all in the motivation. How to motivate, that's the problem. You are the teacher, Emmie."

"What drove you and Mama?"

"No choice, Emmie, only way we had. Education and self-employment. Our generation paid—some overpaid—for our achievements."

"Every generation pays, Robert. They just pay differently."

"It's the taxpayers who are paying to retrain your dropouts. High priced, too."

"Don't start in on Emmie. It isn't her fault that the kids come out of high school unable to read and write."

"I have some very good writers in my class."

"See, Robert. You listen to Emmie."

Papa shivers, gets up, takes up the pillow he sits on. "I'll put the air conditioning on. I don't want to sleep in the damp. I had enough of that."

"Let's talk about something else, Emmie, don't forget to speak to Bernie. We would like to see you for Passover."

"I will, Mama."

"Emmie, do you want to sleep in the guest room tonight?"

"I could if you like."

"You wouldn't have to get up so early that way. The cleaners will be at the guest cottage at about 8:00."

"No sense having to change the linens again. Wait breakfast for me. Goodnight, Mama, Dad. I'm going to call Bernie."

"You can call from here."

"Let her be, Millie, she wants to talk to Bernie without us listening."

"After eleven years of marriage."

I kiss Mamma on the forehead, kiss Papa. She asks, "Anything special you want for breakfast?"

"No, thanks, Mama."

"See you in the morning."

"Bernie, I think my Dad is disturbed about the war coming. Bernie, what can I do about that?"

"I don't know, Emmie."

"You're the doctor."

"I'm an ophthalmologist, a pathologist, not a world fixer."

"That's what the world needs, Bernie, a fixer."

"That's more in the domain of social scientists."

"Bernie, write it down: I'll be home tomorrow at four-twelve. Bernie, I miss you."

"What happened?"

"We were talking about the Korean War, just Dad and I, and he just got up, wouldn't talk about the war."

"That's not complex, Emmie. That's avoidance. He put it all away, sets it aside. This Gulf crisis, the call-up of the reserves—Dad is forced to remember things he wants to forget."

"Now you are psychiatrist."

"Not a very good one."

"Bernie, getting old, it's not easy."

"Time enough for that."

"I was talking about my folks."

"I don't think of your folks as old."

"I can see it on Mama, on Dad. I have been here almost two weeks. We have been out to dinner twice, to lunch twice."

"Maybe they are waiting for a rain before they would leave the beach."

"Bernie, I don't want to get old."

"Children will keep you young, Dr. Kramer."

"I know you are right, Bernie. Just one time I want to see if I can make a difference. Two, three years, Bernie, that's all."

"Did you tell your folks?"

"Yes. A few years and they are grandparents."

"No guarantees, Emmie."

"Guaranteed to try. Don't make promises to your folks."

"I'll make a best efforts promise."

"Emmie."

"Don't worry so much, Bernie. Having children is just a normal physiological process."

"Yes, at age twenty-one."

"Not to worry, Dr. Schwartz, leave it to Dr. Kramer. I'll be delighted to be in your arms, Bernie."

"You made a pun, a funny."

"Sex cuts down on stress, Bernie. Write it down."

Through the kitchen window I could see Dad sitting in his rocker, watching CNN. His left hand had been twitching. I could see that with Dad's right hand he was pulling his left hand back. That's the way Dad controls the muscle spasms in his fingers. His thumb is the worst offender. I have seen his left thumb twitch, contract into his palm. I have seen the sweat form on Dad's forehead, seen him grab the thumb, bend the fingers back, and then force his left hand back, back, holding his fingers so that they could not contract and spasm.

Momma sits at the dining room table sorting the family photographs, hundreds in albums from the forties to the nineties. Mama's face is towards me. She is not the thin Mama of the past. Her face is fuller, her lids heavier. "It's harder for me to work on the books at night." So Mama sorts photos into decades. Papa says less and less, hardly says a word to Edith and Erna unless it's business. So, quietly, the fingers back, he then forces his left hand back. I wanted to put my arms around them, kiss them, tell them I understand. Instead, I went in, asked, "Mom, may I have some ice cream?

"I was thinking of that, too, Emmie."

"Ice cream, Dad, low fat, Weight Watchers chocolate."

"Just a couple of tablespoons."

Mama is spooning the portions. "I wish I had your dad's control. Dad can still fit into the pinks he bought in 1950."

"What are 'pinks'?"

"That was part of Dad's dress uniform, pink-tan trousers and green jacket."

"I didn't know that."

"What's to know?"

"About the war and Papa."

"Emmie, are you all packed?" Mama removed war

from the family conversation. Mama shut off the television, the Gulf war disappeared.

In the predawn the CNN television war was there, the television the only light source in the living room. Dad on the floor doing his back roll. Mama in the living room so she could watch the Gulf war, coffee cup in hand, waiting for the sun to rise at seven-twelve. Through the grey predawn mist I jogged to the lighthouse and back. Mom and Dad were on the porch reading *The New York Times*, waiting for me to breakfast.

"It's coming."

"What's coming."

"More tanks, more troops, more artillery, more transports getting ready, not like in Korea. When the First Cavalry landed at Pohan-dong we had no tanks. We had to retreat to Kumchan." On the signal from Mama, just the sideways shake of her head, *No, No,* and a finger to her mouth, I changed the subject, and when I looked again Mom had cupped her hands over her ears. Papa hadn't noticed. He had begun to write on the yellow legal pad. He was writing and listening to the surf sounds, watching the gulls. He sat, the green "Tree Farm" cap pulled down to shade his eyes from the morning sun.

My Uncle Will had his opinions about Dad. "Your dad is compulsive, always has been. What compels your dad to sit and write like that hour after hour? You would think there was someone waiting to read, to produce a hit play, to publish what he writes. Your dad can't get it through his head there aren't three people in all of God's world who give a damn whether he finishes that play of his today or tomorrow or never."

Even if that is true, so what? Dad has every right to do what he wishes. "Writing keeps Dad very busy," is what Mom says.

"Dad, am I interrupting?"

"No. It's our last morning."

"There will be other days. I'll try to come home for Passover."

"I know you will."

"What are you writing?"

"Just a play."

"What about?"

"About three adult daughters and their father who have recently lost their mother, in an automobile accident. It's their first Christmas together without their mother."

"Sounds sad."

"It isn't."

"What happens?"

"Nothing much."

"So, what is it about?"

"It's about continuing to live, how the responsibilities of life, of living, are transferred from generation to generation."

"Heavy, Papa, heavy."

And Papa laughed. "Wait until you see *Sunrise at Seven-Twelve* performed. 'Robert Redford in his most demanding role, as the aging father.' You will see. It's not without hope."

"Mama tells me you are planning to go home about the first of February."

"Passover is early this year. Your Mama wants to get the taxes out of the way before Passover."

"Papa, will you take care of yourself? Go see the rheumatologist."

"You are beginning to sound like your mother."

"You haven't been listening to Mama."

"What did she tell you?"

"Maybe I wasn't to tell you."

"If it's about me, I should be the first to know."

"Mama said the V.A. called, invited you to join a special counseling group for P.O.W.s"

"Too old, Emmie, too old to join anything."

"Mama says the group could help you."

"I was doing pretty well until the Gulf war came into our living room.

"Mama says—"

"Mama shouldn't have called the V.A. They didn't know we were in Florida."

"Mama says—"

"Your mother says too much."

"She means well."

"Who doesn't?"

"I am sorry if I disturbed you."

Papa, I have heard the tone of your last shortened sentence. The more disturbed Papa becomes, the less he says. If he is truly in pain, he goes off by himself, limping down the beach, bent over, swinging his left leg. Before he comes up the four steps to the cottage, Dad stops, throws his shoulders back, straightens out, fixes his smile. That's what Papa did, prepared for his walk, turned, reached for his white socks, his Nike walkers, his Accutron wristwatch. "I'll be back in forty-five minutes."

"Early lunch today, Robert. Emmie has to be at the airport by one."

"I know."

"Papa, can I go with you?"

"You jogged this morning."

"Papa, I would like to, please."

"O.K., Emmie, come along."

"Emmie, make sure your dad doesn't forget to come home by 11:00, no later."

In full sun we walked east on the low tide beach, on the soft smooth sand, past the gulls that rose, when we approached, to swoop over the surf and then settle behind us. One laughing gull did not fly off with the others. He stood on his right leg, turned his head to us. My father bent to the gull, was talking to the gull in sounds that were more hisses than whistles. He told me, "I said, 'Good morning.' Emmie, this is the second year since that gull lost his left leg. Completely rehabbed except for his social relationships with his peers. This gull is always on the outside of the group. His family flies off, he stays. Not for him to join the crowd."

"Wise old bird."

"The handicapped learn."

We walked east until a cut in the sands where a backwater pool had invaded. The surf rose into the pool and then retreated with the tide. "Wait when the surf goes out. We can cross without getting our shoes wet."

I had taken my shoes off. "Papa, do you want me to help you to take off your shoes."

"No, I'll wait." Dad on his heels, his toes pointed upward, wades through the retreating surf at the shallowest, narrowest point. I said, "You didn't get wet."

"Not at all. The tide will be farther out when we come back."

"Isn't this far enough?"

Dad had slowed from a brisk walk to slower than a stroll. "I'd like to make the lighthouse, sort of a first for me. First time this year to the lighthouse. First time my daughter has gone for a walk with me."

"Didn't Edith or Erna go?"

"Not that far."

"I thought . . ."

"Next year you can assign walking with your old father among yourselves, Edith on Monday, Erna on Wednesday. You can have Friday, Saturday, or Sunday."

"Don't be cruel, Papa. That's a lousy joke."

"I wasn't joking."

"Don't get bitter on me."

"Bitter? Me, bitter? Never! Cynical, yes. I'm too smart to get bitter. Bitter just eats your own guts out. I'm not one for killing myself, not after I have come this far."

At the lighthouse park Dad went to the bathroom. I waited. "At my age, Emmie, can't afford to go by a urinal without a peepee."

"Don't get gross, Dad."

"Not gross, just fact. Last week our island police insisted that one of our French tourists put on her bikini top, right here, went out on the beach to inform her." Papa was giggling. "That's what the police do, keep our island free of topless bathers."

"Sounds like you are leading the good life, Papa."

"Early retirement, good pension—it can't be beat."

"Papa, tell me, why do you write?"

"Gives me something to do."

"Be serious, Papa."

"You don't want to know."

"I do, I do."

"You are too young."

"That's unfair, Papa."

"You are right, Emmie," and Papa laughed. "And if I don't tell you, you may never know."

"O.K., Papa, tell daughter."

"It's a way to get ready for death. The story of life is to get ready for a good death."

"What's a good death, Papa?"

"Without whining, without complaining."

"Papa," and then I began to cry.

"Don't cry, Emmie. That's what the army does, teaches you to die without bitching." Then Papa laughed. "Of course, like all education, it's not always successful."

We talked about nothing much on the way back.

Lunch was cottage cheese and yogurt and no conversation. Papa watched FNN, then switched to CNN. Momma watched Papa and I watched Mama and Papa.

"Get dressed, Robert." Papa was in his morning mode, tan walking shorts, sandals, and his red T-shirt, the one with "Iowa Writers Workshop Summer Program 1986" inscribed in white. Papa cleared the breakfast dishes, made no move to get dressed.

"Robert, get dressed. Go like that if you want to. I'm going to leave in exactly forty minutes."

I sat leafing through the albums. I was in the fifties pictures of Edith, Erna in sunsuits, in snowsuits, Mama pulling both on a sled . . . No pictures of Papa with Edith or Erna. Papa had taken the pictures.

"You all packed, Emmie?"

"All packed, and I stripped the bed."

"You didn't have to. The cleaning crew could do it."

"Mama, there are no pictures of Papa."

"Your father threw them all out, every picture of him in his uniform, threw them out when he resigned his commission.

"I didn't know that."

"The year you were born."

"Why would he do that?"

"He'll tell you."

Papa had heard. "Idiots made me do it. The idiots were talking about defending against a nuclear war, putting in air raid shelters in the schools, storing food and water for after the 'bomb,' as if anyone could survive. So I resigned."

"Why did you tear up your photos?"

"It seems pretty extreme now. Then it was one man's protest against an army that talked nuclear war."

"Robert, if you are not ready I am going to go without you."

"'Hush, little baby, don't you cry, Papa is going to . . .'"

"Robert, why don't you stay home. I'll take Emmie to the airport. I'll come right back. I can get my meat at Jerry's. What's a dollar or two more?" Mama goes out the door and I follow. Papa is into his routine, brushing his teeth.

Mama drives across the causeway east, the back windows down so that the wind doesn't undo Mama's hair, not that she has her hair set when she is in Florida, not like when she is in Rock City where she has a standing Friday noon appointment at Ralph's for a wash and trim as needed. Mama keeps her hair very short. "Easier to dry. After all, I swim every day." Mama doesn't have a grey hair; neither do any of her daughters, not yet anyway. Papa is grey hair all over, moustache, chest, and the fringes around his ears. "Maybe it's best Papa didn't come. It won't do your dad any harm to be alone for a couple of hours. I wanted to talk to you, anyway. If it's too hard for you to come home for Passover, I'll understand. I'll explain to Dad."

"Bernie . . . you know Bernie, Mama. Once he starts on an experiment he doesn't like to take time off. I did tell Bernie. Truthfully, Mama, we should go to the Schwartz's. They deserve equal time."

"I'll explain it to Dad. You do what is best for you."

"Mama, Edith could make the Seder. That would be easier for you. You wouldn't have to take the Passover dishes up and down."

"I would do it anyway, Seder or not."

"Mama, you are driving too fast."

"That's what your dad says."

"Mama, you were up to 63 in a 55 mph zone."

"I'll watch it. I don't want any more speeding tickets. Dad wouldn't like it."

"Your generation is showing, Mama: 'Dad wouldn't like it.' "

Mama parked in the handicap zone, put the wheelchair placard on the windshield. "I'll go in with you, see how long you will be delayed."

"You don't have to. I'm a big girl now."

Mama strides. I am behind her. She strides up to the TV console, looks. "On time, Emmie."

The departure lounge at the Southwest Regional Airport is up the escalator. It's elbows and bodies, suntanned bodies waiting. I put my arms around Mama and kiss her. Mama and I sat in the quietest corner of the lounge. Mama kept looking at her wristwatch.

"Mama, you quit worrying. Papa is going to be fine."

"Is that what Dad told you when you went on the walk with him?"

"Yes."

"Your father is a noble man. Doesn't complain to his daughters, keeps all his complaints for me."

"Mama—"

"I'm not your dad's mother, I am his wife."

"At least you don't have three children to take care of."

Mama laughed. "Time took care of that, thank God. At my age I don't even know if I can run after a grandchild."

"Don't you worry, Mama, you will."

"I'll be seventy years old before you have that baby."

"Grandpa lived to be eighty-six."

"That's not so far off."

"Don't you talk that way. Dad doesn't."

"He does to me."

"What is troubling Papa?"

"Same as always. Dad is afraid of dying. He never says it that way. He says, 'Millie, I feel like when I came home to you and the girls, like I was going to die.' "

"How do you answer that, Mama?"

"You have to be tough with your Dad. I told him, 'Don't be dramatic, Robert. It's only a little war in the Middle East. You had your wars. Each generation has its own wars. We made it before, and we are going to make it again.' "

"That help?"

"That's all I can do. He won't go to group. He doesn't think he needs it."

"He would have other P.O.W.s to talk to."

"That's why Dad won't go, doesn't want to talk about it."

Then there was the announcement. "TWA flight to Kansas City and San Francisco . . ." Mama kissed my forehead, strode off. I watched, and she turned and waved from the escalator.

It was in Kansas City that the message was waiting for me. "Emma Schwartz, call you father."

"Your mama is dead. Died in a crash on Lake Park Road, just cross 41."

"How, Papa, how?"

"Mama ran headlong into a truck. The truck driver swears Mama crossed over the median. It was just beyond the curve. Stupid part is if I had gone with Mom I would have been driving. She would have gone shopping in town. That's all on four-lane divided highway."

"Oh, Dad, what do you want me to do?"

"Come home."

"Have you reached Edith?"

"Yes."

"Erna?"

"I left a message on her machine."

Dad was at the airport waiting for me. "We're leaving for Rock City in an hour. The funeral is tomorrow morning."

When Erna came to Rock City it was I who went to the airport to get Erna. Papa had asked me to go. Usually, of course, he went, so that he could speak to each of us alone, for the ten minutes we drove across the Rock River bridge, made a left at the mall and came down the river road and up the bluff to home. When Erna came home, Mama was dead, forever, in her coffin to be buried, waiting for her daughters to bury Mama on the wind swept Iowa knoll.

It has been two months since Mama was buried, two months since I have been home. Papa sits in my living room reading *The New York Times*. Papa no longer comments. He doesn't talk about Mama. He doesn't mention Erna. He watches CNN but doesn't speak about the Gulf war, so I tell myself, *It hasn't been long enough for Papa to recover*. Sometimes I blame Erna for Mama's death. She hurt Mama so. I don't say Mama committed suicide, but Mama was thinking about how Erna spoke to Papa and that distracted Mama and that is why she crossed over the road markings to hit the truck head on. Mama had been driving for forty years without an accident, so it had to be that she had something on her mind, something that was troubling her.

It's Papa's fault, too. Papa should have gone with Mama, taken her out to lunch, shopping. That way Papa was very selfish, did only what he wanted, sat there and wrote, but Mama didn't mind that or she would have said, "Robert, now come along."

Next year, or the very next time Erna says anything unkind, ungenerous to Papa, I'll tell her, "Erna, that kind of talk is unacceptable. You are hurting Papa."

Erna will go back to Paris and not call and not write to Papa. Then Papa will write to her, and call her.

And I'll tell Papa, "Leave Erna alone. It's her problem. She has to work it out herself."

"Emmie, Erna is my daughter."

"Papa, Erna needs help."

"Erna needs a support system, to ventilate to. I learned that in the prison camp."

And when he says that I'll ask him, "Papa, tell me about the prison camp, about the scars."

Chapter 3

Emma

Papa came to Palo Alto in May, stayed a couple of days with us. That's when I read Papa's play, *Sunrise at Seven-Twelve*, versions I, II, and III. In version I, written before Mama died, the mother in the play is already dead when the play begins. I couldn't talk to Papa about his play. "Papa, you wished Mama dead."

"No, Emmie, it's only a play, a story about a family, of aging. Of three daughters and two cottages on the Florida Gulf coast."

Thank God Bernie is a listener. "Bernie, I want to talk to Papa about his play. You read it. The mother is dead, only a memory, an ever present memory."

Bernie read the play. "O.K., Emmie, your dad is afraid of dying, so he transfers his death to Mama. That doesn't mean he wished her dead. My God, Emmie, you can't believe that."

"I still had to talk to Papa." I did when we were alone. "Bernie may be right about the transference. I don't know a damn thing about death wishes. Never had a course in psych. The only psychiatrist I ever met was at the V.A. That was years ago. The only thing he talked about was sex."

"Papa."

"Emmie, please don't drive so fast."

"I'm only keeping up with traffic."

"Sorry, Emmie. I shouldn't be telling you how to drive."

"Papa, are you sleeping all right? I heard you up two, three times during the night."

"All old men do that."

"Would you like to come to California for the winter. You don't have to stay with us. I could always find a rental for you."

"I have been thinking about that since Mama died. I would rather we all be together in Florida. That's what Florida was to Mama, a place for the family to be together."

"Things have changed, Papa."

Papa stayed a couple of days, then he went down to Sana Monica to see Uncle Will and Aunt Anne. Two, three weeks after Dad returned to Rock City, Bernie had an ophthalmology meeting in Los Angeles. We stopped off in Santa Monica. My Uncle Will, Dad's brother, is six years older than Dad, seventy-five. He is still straight and tall, with only a little bald on the top, only a tinge of grey at the temple. Will looks like what he was, a retired "show biz exec" in pastel shades of California colors slacks and sport coats.

"Why does Uncle Will look younger than you, Dad?"

"That's simple, Emmie. He was never self-employed." That was my father answer to me when I was a little girl. Twenty years later I am almost sure what Dad said in jest could very well be truth and wisdom. Bernie was at his meeting. To be alone with Uncle Will, I jogged with him, he in nylon green and yellow jogging suit doing his heel and toe power walk on the sidewalk that follows the Santa Monica Beach to Venice. "Emmie, you ought to get new Balance walking shoes. They come in assorted widths. Your shoes may be O.K. for tennis, but you need walking shoes."

All the Kramers have opinions. It's not only Uncle Will and Dad; it's thir generation. Advise and care of wives and daughters like in the *shtetl* in Poland.

"Uncle Will," we were stopped at a red light waiting for the walk signal, "how do you think Dad is getting along?"

"Bobby is a damn fool; now he is a dramatist, a screen writer, wasting his life again. What does he know from plays?

From real estate he knows, and not that much, either. If Bobby is a playwright, I'm Little Red Riding Hood. I read his play, all about a grandchild that isn't all together, and on her your father places the whole future of the family."

"It doesn't sound like the same play I read."

"That's your dad. No wonder no one publishes his work. Crazy. Our Uncle Harry noticed that sixty years ago. You never knew our Uncle Harry, may he rest in peace."

Uncle Will has the same virtue as Dad. Ask him one question, you get an autobiography.

"You tired, Emmie?"

"No."

"O.K., we'll turn around."

"You were telling me about Uncle Harry."

"Harry, may he rest in peace, was my mama's brother-in-law."

"So?"

"Oh yes. Harry always said, "Is *felt* Bobby a *Klepke*?"

"What?"

"You don't understand Yiddish. That'a shame, such a colorful language. It means 'The clapper is missing from your bell.' Like you are not a hundred percent in the head."

"How old was Papa when he left home?"

"About twenty when the war started."

"Did he change much?"

"No, not until after Korea."

"What happened then?"

"Ran out of guts. I told him, 'Bobby, you come to California, that's where it's at, not in Rock City.' In Rock City he is a big man. Here he would have been a millionaire. Look at our house, a little bungalow I bought for forty thousand. We added on a couple of rooms; now it's worth more than three hundred thousand."

"Dad did pretty well."

"*Bobkes* he made."

"What?"

"*Bobkes*: small turds, garbage. Your mama, may she rest in peace, she made more money buying those two cottages on the Gulf than your father did in thirty years of 'developing.' No guts. I told him, 'Bobby, I'll help you come out.' What does he answer? 'In Rock City I know what I have.'

"I told him when he was here, 'Bobby, sell those *Kokamamie* properties, go for a cruise, meet someone, go out, enjoy.' "

"Dad enjoys what he does."

"He should have been an artist. He was a very good artist. So, he goes to college. First in the family to go to college. So he ends up in Korea."

"Mama never told me, but there were hints Papa had problems when he came home from Korea."

"Your mama never told you? I'll tell you. My brother Bobby thought he was going to die. Why he would think he was going to die after he came home, after the POW camp? This I never understood. It took him a year to get his act together. Your mother was a saint. I am going for a shower, Emmie."

"Uncle Will, do you think Dad is managing O.K.?"

"He'll survive. At our age we survive."

Book II

Chapter 4

Edith

Frank and I have been married for twenty-one, going on twenty-two, years. Although Frank does have an orderly mind, I have never ascribed any particular wisdom to his business acumen. "Edith," he says to me after reading my dad's letter, "you had better go down to Florida before the Kramer Companies' annual meeting. You are the oldest daughter — you should be protecting your parents," which, of course, means I should be protecting my interests, so that my sister Erna doesn't get more than her fair share from Dad's Kramer Companies.

It's not really fair to say my dad's; my mother would be the first to tell you. "Your dad and I worked together for forty years. We had a partnership. I did the day-to-day, and Dad did the long range planning. Kramer Companies are what is left of the partnerships after the IRS, the corporate dissolution, eleven years of real estate non-market in western Illinois, and Dad's one hundred percent loss of his investment in the Bank of New England."

My husband, Frank, is orderly, persistent, and annoyingly repetitive. "Edith, now you are the oldest, so you make sure. You have the education. Edith, go through the monies due your folks, the will changes, review them with your mom and dad, explain it to them if you have to. Make sure they understand what they are doing. Once they go, you can't correct their errors and omissions." That admonition is based on Frank's one and only experience with estate planning, when his uncle George died. Uncle George had no children. Frank's sister, Georgia, named after "rich" Uncle George, got the farm, and we got a half share of the house in town. This after fourteen Christmases at our house when Uncle George always said, "Frank I left everything equal to you and your sister Georgia." Georgia was the one who went with Uncle to Abbott, Abbott and Abbott just four months before he died. I have never said anything to Frank, but based on my experience in our bank's trust department, there are lawyers in Rock County who, for an inducement or a suggestion or for the hope of future relationships, will follow the instructions of the beneficiary and not the will maker's.

"I am sure it was our uncle's intent for me to have the farm." That is what Georgie told Frank, when for the last four Christmases all Uncle George would talk about while he was looking out the window was his experiences as a marine in World War I. "The first day we got into the trenches at Bellau Wood it was so quiet you could hear the crows. When the fighting started, there wasn't a bird left in the sky." That's how it was last Christmas.

"Uncle George, more cranberry sauce?"

"Edith, I didn't get to Paris until 1919."

Frank did get half the family photographs. It took almost a year to sell the house. As Ralph Hansen, our attorney, said at the closing (Ralph, Frank and I all went to Rock City High school together), "I am sorry, Frank. I'm sure your uncle meant what he said to you, but that is not what was written in the will."

Georgia is not stupid; she didn't take Uncle George to

Ralph Hansen. She found Abbott, her school board crony. To placate Frank, I told him, "You know Papa is very careful about his personal affairs," which is a euphemism for Dad's *investment achievements*. "If your dad had spent as much time watching his investments as avoiding taxes, your dad would not have lost so much of our money," is what Frank answered.

"O.K., I'll go . . . I'll go."

Dad writes once a week; the first part of the letter is full of Florida local color: "Saw a dolphin flipping his tail off shore, so close I could have waded out on the sandbar and touched him. There were two mergansers in the surf, quite unusual. First time in our sixteen years on this Gulf shore that I have seen that species of ducks in the surf. Yesterday, Mom and I drove through the Bird Sanctuary. The roseate spoonbills were wading, feeding in the pools not thirty feet from us."

Then the second part. "Dear Edith,

"Erna would like to come out on January 1," then something about that being a slow time at her restaurant, "so how about a family meeting that week? Emma says it's fine; she called yesterday. All O.K.

"Love, Mom and Dad."

Frank read the letter. "That's settles that, Edith."

"Why does it have to be when Erna wants?"

"Ask your dad."

From Dad the answer is always the same. Edith, with your seniority at the bank you can take off whenever and Emma won't have to teach until the 10th and Michael and Erna . . . *Well, you know how it is in a restaurant six days a week. They work so hard . . . running a French restaurant in San Francisco in today's economy.*

"What did your dad say?"

"Dad said the usual: Michael and Erna have been slaving over a hot skillet, working day and night just to pay for their green Jaguar and their condo in the highrise with a view of the Golden Gate Bridge. Dad said 'Edith, what harm will it do for us to all be together when it's best for Erna?' " which Frank finishes: "As long as Erna keeps getting handouts from your dad, she and Michael will never report a profit."

"Dad is keeping a record of what Erna is getting so that all comes out equal at the end."

"That's what he intends to do. You be sure he is doing exactly that."

"How?"

"Go down a week ahead of time, make sure."

That, of course, is what I did, went down to Florida the day after Christmas. Dad and Mom are at the Southwest Regional Airport. Dad is tanned, walking just a little straighter; Mom is beside him, cane in hand, striding faster that he does. Both look more relaxed, younger than when they stopped off in Chicago for Thanksgiving with us. Dad drove, with the sliding roof open to the wind and sunshine, and Mom talked. "We have been fixing up the guest cottage for Emmie and Erna. You can stay with us."

"Bought a new refrigerator, a new mattress, new curtains." That's Dad, finishing Mom's sentence as he always has. I don't know how she can stand that.

"Don't do too much—wait until Frank comes down. He'll help you."

"There will be enough for Frank to do."

Dad is nonstop on his month's achievements. "I caulked the bathroom and around the kitchen cabinets. "Burger is finally going to pay us. He pays March eight on the first note. In 1999 we get the second note paid off. We have had an offer on the guest cottage . . .

"If we sell both cottages, we can almost triple our long term bond investments."

Then my mom finishes that part of Dad's report. "Robert, the cottages are mine."

"So they are, Millie, to do with as you wish. I was only bragging on your astuteness, your wisdom in choosing to invest in Gulfshore cottages rather than in bank stock."

My mother answers with her usual charm, "Robert, it was you who made our cottages possible, and that did turn out better than your shares in the Bank of New England."

To which Dad asks, "How's Frank?" and follows with, "How's your career going, Edith? Erna will be here on the first."

I don't answer and Dad doesn't notice.

"When is Emma coming?"

"Didn't I tell you?"

"Tell me what?"

"Didn't I write to you?" That's another habit of my dad's, answering a question with a question, and never letting Mom finish a sentence, which makes conversation with my father most difficult.

"Dad, when is Emma coming?"

"When is Emma coming?" This is Dad to Mom.

"The seventh, Robert. You have to pick Emmie up at eleven ten on the seventh.

I remember that night: After supper Mom is settling down with Gabriel Garcia Marquez, and Dad is in his rocker with The New York Times. I tried again.

"Dad."

"Yes, Edith."

"I spoke to Jim Horst, one of our trust officers."

"What about, Edith?"

"About estate planning." Estate planning is the way to gain Dad's attention.

"What about?"

"If you and Mom have been giving anyone of us more than twenty thousand a year, you have to file a gift tax report." Which is a nice way of saying that there will be a record for me to review.

"Peat Marwick will do that for me."

Doing so well with one answer, I tried for two. "Dad, you don't always have to do what Erna wants, not all the time. It's not the duty of the Kramer family to support her restaurant."

"They have been working so hard."

"We all work hard, Dad."

"They took a risk, put everything they had into the restaurant. So much invested without help, they could lose it all."

"Who helped you and Mom?"

"Who was there who could help us?"

There he goes again, a question with a question.

"Dad, there is risk in our careers. Frank and I have more than twenty years invested in our jobs, and look where we are. When you and Mom had been in business for twenty years, look what you had. Our generation will never have what you had at your age, a fine house, an art collection."

"Debt is what we had."

"Don't go poor mouthing, Dad. It doesn't fit your lifestyle."

"Sorry, Edith, what were you saying about Erna?"

"What I was saying is I know you intend to treat each of us equally —" Again Dad doesn't let me finish.

"But what if you had a special need, what am I to do then?

What if you needed extra cash when you were putting the addition on your house and you came to me."

"Listen to me, Dad. What I am saying is the more you give Erna, the more she will spend."

"How do you know that?"

The only answer I could come up with is, "If you

didn't give her everything she asked for, she could live like Frank and me."

"How is that, Edie?"

When Dad calls me Edie he is turning back forty years when there was only one Kramer girl, Edith Anne, just Dad and Edith in his rose garden, me beside him on the gravel, while he cut and pruned and mulched his Sunday afternoons away. "Edie, you remember the first office duplex we ever built, the one on Fourth Avenue. I went by there. The pin oak in the back yard must be sixteen feet tall. You remember you helped me plant it." That was the first time. That became our logo, our trademark. Kramer Construction, pin oaks planted at every project we ever did. "Edie, we planted twelve hundred oak, red white, and walnut, all on six acres on the farm. In forty years you'll have the finest hard wood timber growth in Western Illinois."

"Dad, I'm forty-six. In forty years I'll be eighty-six."

"May you live to be a hundred and twenty."

"Dad."

"Yes, Edie, yes."

"Dad, you don't have to support free enterprise in San Francisco. You don't have to support Erna's and Michael's restaurant."

"It hasn't been easy for them."

"Dad, nothing is easy for anyone. It's not easy for Frank; it's not easy for me."

"How are things at the bank, Edie?"

"Let me finish, Dad. For all you know, Erna and Michael may be—I want to put it nicely, Dad—Erna and Michael may be diverting your monies into other investments or spending it."

Mama heard our conversation. Mama spoke up—I remember that. "You listen to her, Robert. Edith has a good head. She understands business and risk."

"So, why didn't she come home and help us run our business?"

"Robert, you wouldn't have listened to Edith. Only fights is what we would have had. We would have lost a daughter. You never listened to me. You wouldn't. You never listened. You didn't listen to Edith when Edith told you about the Bank of New England."

"All Edith said was, 'Dad, you shouldn't have so much of your portfolio in one stock.' "

"Not then, Robert. When Edie told you to sell, when you still could have made a profit."

"Not a profit."

"Not a loss, Robert, not a complete wipeout, zero, nothing."

"Mama, that's not entirely fair. Dad called the bank. The bank lied to Dad, told him all would work out."

"Your dad believed the Bank of New England and not you."

"Did you expect the truth from—"

Dad paused, put down *The New York Times*. "We always ran our business on truth."

"Dad."

"I know you mean well, Edie. You'll see how difficult it is to reach decisions. I'm not Solomon. I'm just Robert Kramer trying to do the best for three daughters."

"Don't apologize, Dad. That's what I'm trying to tell you: You done good, Dad. You don't have to do better.

"You'll see, Edith, when you'll take over, it's not easy."

I shouldn't have gotten angry, but I did. "We are not talking about you and your dying. Whenever I talk to you, you turn it around to talk about yourself. I was talking about Erna, and Emma, and me, Papa." When I say Papa, I'm that one little girl again, alone with my dad in the park before I became Edith the oldest and he became Dad.

"All this would have never happened."

"This? What's *this*, Robert? Tell me what are you talking about?"

Mom had trouble hearing from across the room. Dad had turned more toward to me in the armchair beside the rocker . . . . .I hadn't planned to get Mama into this. After fifty years of business, Mama wanted to discuss contemporary literature and not taxes. Mom I was saving as the the approval giver, at worst as the arbitrator. God forbid, if it came to it, the peacemaker between Edith Kramer and her father.

"Robert, what are you saying?"

"I'm saying if we would have grandchildren, one, two, three grandchildren, all right, even one grandchild from each daughter, we could have given all the money away, twenty thousand to each grandchild, in no time at all. No estate taxes, no conversations where all we speak about is money. Has any one of my daughters ever talked to me, 'Papa, tell about how things were, or tell me about how things were when you and Mom got started, tell me what it was like.' You never even asked your mother what it was like for her all alone with me in the army. She alone with you, and alone again when I got called up for the Korean War, alone with you and Erna. Look at TV today, interviews with the families whose husbands are in Saudi Arabia. Edie, did you ever ask me once, 'Dad, why did you and Mom go into business, take all those risks?' You ever ask us the price Mom and I paid for being part of the free enterprise system?"

"You chose it."

"Don't be cruel, Edith. Your father isn't feeling well."

"Don't put the guilt on me, Mom. I'm forty-six years old.

You don't have to tell me what to say." That's as far as far as I got that evening. Frank may be correct: "Protect yourself, Edith. No one else will." But peace in a family is more important. Mom never mentioned Dad is not feeling well again. I tried to take Dad for a walk: "Dad, you want to walk up to the lighthouse with me?"

"Dad walked enough."

I tried when I saw Dad taking a pill with his dinner.

"Only pain and spasm, a little sciatica, a little rheumatism."

"Do the pills help?"

"Not much, Edie."

When mama was alive, she guarded Papa. Now he guards himself with silence. It's when I think of what Dad said about grandchildren, that I must remember that it has taken me six years and then seven months of one on one counseling to accept that Frank and I can't have children, and as Frank said, we aren't going to adopt, either. To accept that Erna is aggressively manipulative in pursuing her own interests, that has only taken me three years to realize. For me, that is a satisfactory rate of reality perception. How I relate to my dad that I'm working on. I should have, I should have told Mom and Dad years ago, "Frank and I want children." If I had said, "We can't have children, but we have tried, tried for years," I know my father or even Moma would have said it, "You can adopt." That's why I didn't tell them. Frank won't adopt. He has studied the risks; he won't adopt. *Why, it's all in the genes, Mama. It's in the research, it's all inherited depression, alcoholism.* "Edith, your uncle Larry, may he rest in peace, a depressive alcoholic, on Mama's side half the family was depressive. They managed." With my father, he has to have the last word, so I never told him. I should have told him. *Papa, Mama, I have heard your story, emigrant boy works his way through college selling Fuller Brushes, so poor, we lived on eight dollars a week.* ◻ "When your father was in the army it was lucky I had a good job. Times were different then.

When your father came home, then Jews couldn't get jobs in industry, in banking. Whoever heard of jobs in banking? All right, a few of our friends worked for the government, and the farm machinery industry, they always employed Jewish engineers, but for us, we were left with self-employment. We never wanted very much, just a living."

You done good, Mama, Papa. You educated your children, you supported the synagogue, you gave to every social agency in town. Your names are on bronze plaques. For Christmas you get cards of Happy New Year from the residents of Elder House built by the Kramer Companies. You done good, Papa. You never had a labor law violation, you didn't discriminate, you didn't fight OHSHA, not even when it cost you. You were tolerant of your partners who stole from you. You were patient with your adversaries; you didn't hate your foe. You went to services in the morning. When you die, Papa, your picture will be on the front page of the *Rock City Gazette*. "Developer of first rental housing for families with children in Western Illinois; reserve officer, married for fifty years to the same woman." Times are changing, Papa. It's not that sort of a world anymore. You know why I didn't adopt: All right, Frank's genetic theories didn't help. Papa, what if Frank and I were divorced with a child, how was I going to support a child, continue a career? You would have helped, you were always there. *That's what money is for, Edie, to help to give you choices.* But, Papa, I'm not Erna; for me it's not so easy to take. You made it so easy, but, Papa, I would help you if you would let me. Papa, you are not doing Erna a favor by giving. "That's not so, Edie. It's says in our Jewish tradition if you ask you give, and the living need."

That is your need, Papa, to be needed. You were lucky, Papa, you have three daughters who love you, what have I got, Papa. It's not my fault, Papa, I tried, we tried.

Now, Papa, I'm forty-six; it's all too late. Papa, who will visit me when I'm seventy? Papa, you should not have said grandchild, but I forgive you. I'll talk to Erna, and if Emma will listen, I'll talk to her. Papa, you are entitled to grandchildren. I'm sorry, Papa. But, Papa, I'm not guilty.

Chapter 5

Edith

On New Year's Day afternoon, Erna appeared in her red rented convertible and black Chanel travel suit. Erna pecked us all on the cheek and unloaded her Louis Vuitton case and a Daniel Hector duffel bag full of presents for us. Erna is as tall as I, five feet nine, but much thinner. This I attribute to Michael's French nouvelle cuisine, not her genetic pool. Erna stays thin and straight while I'm approaching the slouching, full-bellied body that Mom so deplored. I hear Mom, "Look at me, see what happens to a woman's body when they get older, Edith. Stand up straight."

"Mama I'm forty-six years old."

In twenty minutes Erna is back from the guest cottage in an all-white tennis outfit with a red diagonal blaze on the pockets, the latest from this year's "in" California sportswear designer collections. Erna is . . .Well, to put it carefully, Erna is not only what she looks like: She is more than the tanned California perfume model. She is much more than that. She is the Stanford MBA with honors who handles spreadsheets, agendas, and, I suspect, the investments for Michael's "reserves," not profits as she insists.

We Kramers are all gathered on the screened porch

facing the Gulf surf. Mama was into The New York Times crossword; Dad writing the weekly Thursday letter to his two property managers. The wind is from the southwest, which makes the surf sounds louder than usual and has moved the pelicans to fish on the bayside of the island.

Mama looked at Erna. "Yesterday, before the storm, there were a dozen pelicans fishing out there. You should have seen the pelicans with the gulls hovering beside them. There were so many fish."

"There are more shells on the beach today because of the storm." That's my dad, always topping Mom. "Edith, tell me how is your career going?"

"On hold, Dad. Everything is on hold."

"In this economy, banks aren't growing. No loan demand and high interest rates takes care of that."

"We took in more than ever at the restaurant, but I expect the yearend financial will show no better than last year."

Hiding your profit in inventory or reserves or are you skimming cash, Erna?

"I surely thought that this year you and Michael would show a profit." That's fairly direct for my dad.

"Michael and I are so grateful to you and Mom. Without you . . ." Erna trails off, lowers her eyes in a style she must have learned from the silent black and white flics of the '20's.

Dad is still exploring. "Erna, how long is your lease?"

"Thank God, another six years."

"Don't thank God, Erna, thank John Krouse, your landlord, for the lowest rent I have ever heard of."

"It was a nothing space, an abandoned store front before Michael realized its possibilities."

"You are not sharing with Mr. Krouse. Equitable commercial leases reserve a percentage share for the landlord."

"Old John is rich enough." Erna laughs. "It took Michael six months before he got John to sign that sweetheart lease." Michael got the rent down that low because, Erna laughs, Michael told him, "Mr. Krause, I'm only going to be open on Thursday, Friday and Saturday. How can I pay a full rent if I am only open three days a week. Mr. Krouse, if I am not open, you don't have to heat. We don't use water. You won't lose a thing."

"Aren't you open six days a week."

"A lease is a lease, Edith. There are no use restrictions to Thursday, Friday, Saturday. John is not happy, but Michael says he is too old, too tired to fight us."

"You may be surprised, Erna. Old John may wake up and haul you off into court, get his justified increases."

"Michael says he is too busy going to the doctor."

Papa had heard the saga of Michael's "triumph."

"Maybe you and Michael would be better off not fighting with Mr. Krouse. He seemed like a very nice man when I met him."

"Papa, we are not fighting. Mr. Krouse brings it up two, three times a year, and you know what Michael says."

"What?"

"Read the lease, Mr. Krouse; you signed it."

Mama hadn't said a word, just sat there listening. "Erna, you could learn from your father about business relationships. It's better to have Mr. Krouse for a friend. With landlords it's best not to fight. The years go by and soon it's time to renew."

"Old John will be dead by then."

"All the more reason to make peace before he dies."

"It's not that kind of a world, Mama; low rent is our competitive edge. We earned it."

Mama didn't impact, so as usual she changed directions. "Why don't you and Edie go for a walk, go look at the sunset. The sunsets have been so beautiful, the clouds all lit up with the sun's reflections. It's been so clear we could see the lights from Marco."

We listened to our mama and walked west into the evening. The surf had quieted. The gulls, the sandpipers, the terns had left the beach. The crows were silent. The low tide beach was covered with the storm's refuse, pen shells and seaweed, pink sponge and empty cans of Budweiser. I turned and saw Dad take Mom's hand to kiss it. I looked at myself beside Erna . . . Edith, your thighs are too heavy. Either get a longer cover-up or don't walk the beach in your three-year-old bathing suit. Edith, you are forty-six years old, you are the oldest. One day you will have to reach the decisions on how to distribute your father's and your mother's estate. That won't be for sixteen years — that's what the actuary said, forty-six and sixteen. I'll be sixty-two. Erna will always need. Emma, unless she changes, will go along with anything. Erna wants and I'll be left to reach decisions neither one will approve of. I will become the domineering oldest sister, if not despised, certainly not appreciated for my Solomonic wisdom. Not yet, Edith, in sixteen years.

About Erna taking from our parents: be resolute, Edith.

Talk to Erna, try. It's for the folks' sake.

"How do the folks look to you?"

"About the same as last year."

"I think Papa . . . Well, Papa doesn't. I don't think his head is as good as it was when he was with me for Thanksgiving."

"You worry too much. He looks fine to me."

"Who is going to worry, you and Emma in San Francisco?"

"You know Mom and Dad are welcome to come to San Francisco. We have very mild winters."

"You know what the cottages mean to Mama and Dad,

too. That's what they look forward to all year, the family getting together."

"They have never invited Michael."

"That's unfair, Erna. Mom did for years. What did she get? 'Too busy, it's our inventory time, have to get ready for this or that.' Always excuses. Mom just gave up on Michael."

"Michael isn't comfortable around Papa."

"Around Papa's Yiddish expressions, about his stories of his life in Poland."

"How can Papa remember he left Poland when he was five or six?"

"We can't refute his memories." I chuckled.

"That's good, Edith, you made a funny, develop your sense of humor, it may help you get over your guilt. Still seeing your shrink?"

"She is not a shrink; she is a counselor."

"Counselor, shrink, she getting you over your guilt? You are just like Papa: guilt, guilt. Papa is going to give too much to his college. Poor Papa, feels guilt about everything, surviving the Holocaust, surviving World War II and Korea, making money when he never intended to. You've heard him: all he wanted was a living, and he went from one project to another. You are just like him, Edith, full of Jewish angst. You feel guilty because you couldn't have children for Papa and Mama. You feel guilty because for ten years Papa has been gifting to you. So, what do you do? Spend it all on addition to your house so Papa and Mama will have 'a room of their own' for their old age, all on one floor with safety treads in the sit-down shower. Grow up, Edith. You are forty-six years old. It's not that kind of a world anymore. Our parents will either die at home with nurses around the clock and if their money runs out, in a county nursing home, incontinent, in adult diapers, simple-minded, tied to a wheel chair."

So I began to cry, and Erna said, "I didn't mean to hurt you, I was only talking about the real world."

"Erna, if you had any sensitivity at all, you know I can't handle . . ."

Erna put her arms around me. "Crying isn't all bad, Edie, I wish I could cry." We walked home very slowly, and once Erna took my hand, and said, "I'm not that stupid, Edie. Being oldest is not easy. I'm glad I don't have your hang-ups about children's obligations to take care of Mama and Papa." And then I thought I heard Erna say, *This world is a bitch, then you die.*

"What did you say, Erna?"

"I said, 'All our timing is wrong.' Here we are, three Kramer girls, into their careers, with parents who may need their care and attention, that at the very time you will be named V. P. for management, Emma will get tenure, and Michael and I will want to move to France."

I nodded and quit crying. I had to rate my first effort to influence Erna as nothing, zero, that after all my planning of what and how to tell Erna I never got to the first phrase, *I'm talking to you because I know how concerned you are about Mom and Dad's future.* The one thing I had learned from my talk with Erna, her retirement to France was already in the planning phase, and that wouldn't have been achieved without Michael's approval because, as my sister Emmie said at Erna's and Michael's wedding, "Erna must see something in Michael Vevers that I don't, or why would she marry a divorced French sous chef with a grown son." Mama had also seen it. "Erna needs someone to orchestrate. For Erna it's not enough that he be successful. She wants to create, to mold — in her image, of course."

Will Michael be eternally grateful for being lifted from sous chef at Le Grandville to chef-owner of Michael's to retired restaurateur. Hometown boy returns to Banyulssur-la-Mer, Pop. 3500 on the Mediterranean Coast, 150 miles north of Barcelona, after successful business career in San Francisco. I would bet Erna won't go back to that Catalonian fishing town no matter how picturesque the plaza. What was the name of the restaurant his folks ran, Chez Rosa? Banyuls or Paris, Erna is not going to be there when the folks need her. Reserves plus advances from Papa equals early retirement. The reason she wants her share sooner than later? To invest in France or Spain. Spain is the growth market since joining the European Economic Community.

Edith, you have a suspicious mind. Based on years of careful observation of my dear sister Erna.

For the next two days the weather turned cool, into the sixties and windy, the skies in the clear sunlight were grey blue. We sat on the porch, my father saying little, writing in his journal, "Just finishing and correcting," joining us with comments. "Sorry, Erna, I don't think that this sky is like a Boudin painting, too much glare in the light here. Florida light is much brighter. Boudin was in northern France. Look at Boudin's sky more closely. Look at the puffs, the layers. Erna, see for yourself the Florida sky is more like what Georgia O'Keefe painted. The series she based on her flights above the clouds."

Erna doesn't answer Papa. She returned to *The New Yorker*, returns to us with a comment, "There is a two-part feature on the life in the New Haven ghetto, drugs, broken families, single mothers, alcoholism. Right down Emma's alley." Erna wrote on cover, "Emma." Dad said nothing. He was too occupied trying to get up. My dad has an arthritis that affects the large muscles of his legs, makes it very difficult for him to get out of his chair unless he has something to support both his arms on. It's by pushing up with his arms that he rises from behind the glass top table that he uses as a desk.

Dad comes back, begins on me. "Keeping a journal, planting a tree . . . so the grandchildren will know."

Again grandchildren. Get grandchildren out of your head, Edith.

I lean over, look at Dad's legal pad. Dad's handwriting is jagged, irregular, angulated.

"Edith, you want to read what I am writing?"

"No, Dad."

"You may if you wish."

"I didn't mean to interrupt you."

"You read, I'll get up, get a drink." Dad makes it a rule to get up out of his armchair with the pillow on the seat once an hour. If he doesn't, Mama reminds him. "Robert, the doctor told you to keep moving." Dad gets up, goes to refrigerator, pours his water, then there is a clatter of ice cubes on the kitchen floor.

"Robert, if you wanted a drink, why didn't you tell me? I would have gotten if for you. Now I have to clean up the floor."

"Millie, I didn't intend to drop the ice tray."

Mama was still on Papa. "You dropped the plastic cap off the milk bottle this morning. You could be more careful."

"You have to understand, Millie. I can't do any better. It was an accident."

"You don't try."

Papa doesn't answer. He is on the kitchen floor, picking up ice cubes, throwing them into the sink. Erna has not gotten up to help. Mama has. She has a towel on the floor, wiping it dry. "You didn't have to do that, Robert. I would have picked up." During the cleanup in the kitchen I read Papa's journal.

Jan. 4. Yesterday Leroy Carlson, Carlson Construction has made another offer for both cottages. Will continue negotiations, explore price and tax free exchange as per Erna's suggestions . . .

Did Papa want me to read what he had written, and why hasn't Dad or Erna or Mama told me? Mom knew everything about her beach cottages. "These are my cottages, Robert. I am the one who bought them so that our family would have a place where we could all be together." Dad was back to his table, Mom was into her crossword, and Erna on her next *New Yorker* that Dad brought down for his "frivolous" reading.

"I love these cool days on the beach." That's what Mama said. "Less humidity on the cool days." Papa.

"Gives us a chance to go shopping. I have to get some bran muffins for Dad. Do you want to go with me, Edith?"

"Mama, why don't you let Edith and me go? Stay home, enjoy."

Erna is driving. That one time she did. I have the shopping list. January is off-season on this too narrow barrier island. The island is twenty miles from east to west with fifty percent reserved for a bird sanctuary. This tropical island, with a population of thirty-five hundred that will become twenty thousand in February. This island, whose voters have a per capita income of eighty-three thousand a year. This island, with six units of assisted housing, whose day visitors pay a three dollar causeway bridge fee. The Australian pines make a shaded bower of the one shopping street. The sign, "Jerry's," in green and white with a white pelican in flight, is small, discrete. The market has covered parking with an elevator to the champagne, wine, bakery, groceries and flowers, a chocolate and fudge bar, plus service counter for newspapers, cigars and stamps. Racks of champagne and wine, unsold for New Year's consumption, are now remarked with pink lables, "Reduced."

"Forty percent's too much for a brand not fit to drink."

That as Erna passes the Totts Champagne. "I brought some Korbel. We will break it out when Emma comes, for after the annual meeting." That's Erna's euphemism for Dad's state of Kramer Companies year-end report to his daughters.

"What are we going to celebrate?"

"A deal of a lifetime, Edith. Next year we could get five times our annual distribution and no one would get hurt, sort of a 1991 Bonus."

"How?"

"Too early to say yet, elder sister. A once in a lifetime opportunity to sell the cottages."

"Those are Mama's cottages."

"Don't worry, Edith. Mom and Dad will be taken care of."

"Mama loves the cottages."

"She will love her condo even more."

"What condo?"

"Hasn't Dad told you?"

"No."

"He will."

"I hope so."

"We will not do a thing without your approval and without Emma's, too."

"Why hasn't Dad said anything to me?"

"He is your father, too. You ask him."

On the way back Erna drove south and then east on the Gulf road. "Not much Gulf front property left, not like when Mom and Dad came to the island . . ." The time shares and the three-story condos with elevators, so far from the beach, so far from the gulls and the terns, and the doves that live under the cape honeysuckle.

"Maybe the real estate slowdown will keep the developers off the island."

"Not a chance, Edith. You know development is the highest and best land use. That's what real estate is all about."

"Too many damn condos. Comes February you won't be able to drive the Gulf road."

"We will be gone by then. The folks will be back in Rock City."

We passed a sign, blue and green and white, "Victoria Cove Cottages by Carlson."

"Leroy Carlson does a good job of marketing."

"You know him that well?"

"Been talking to him."

Leroy Carlson, Carlson Construction in Dad's journal, sale, trade or tax-free exchange. "Developing condos is risky business in this market."

"That's the banker in you talking, Edie."

"Bad real estate loans is why the Bank of New England was taken over by the Federal Deposit Insurance Corporation."

"You worry too much, Edith."

"Somebody has to."

"If you hadn't torn yourself apart, worry, worry, you wouldn't have had all those loose parts to put together."

"Making choices is not easy."

"Now go feeling guilty about Dad's money giving you the opportunity to make choices."

"It's not guilt, Erna. I'm just trying to reach the right choice for everyone."

"Do for yourself. Everyone is impossible."

"We are not all the same, Erna."

"I know we don't all have the same goals."

"Not goals, Edith, needs."

So I didn't pursue "for Mom and Dad's sake." I didn't want to hear Erna's answers. "You sure it isn't for your own sake?"

Edith, you reach great decisions. You manage fifty-four employees at the bank. Today you aren't sure of what is best for Mom and Dad because Erna and Dad are negotiating without you. That doesn't mean you are wrong, Edith Kramer. Why can't you speak up, Edith, straight up? "Dad, Erna, tell me what's the deal with Leroy Carlson? What's in it for you and Mom?"

"Erna, why do you need the money?"

"I'm getting a divorce from Michael."

No explanations. I knew. I had known for years. Mom and Dad knew how Michael beat her. That was why Dad gave Erna the extra money, to permit her to leave Michael. I had never told Frank that Dad had also given me money, "To have if you need." I have those monies at the Sanibel Island Bank, where Erna has been depositing hers for the past eight years. Why should I tell Frank? It's money my dad gave to me alone.

Chapter 6

Edith

Thursday is Dad's telephone day, his effort to keep in touch with Kramer Companies and yet to stay in his vacation mode. Everything in its time, everything in its place, that's the Kramer Family way. Not to interfere with Dad, Erna calls her office from the guest cottage, and I don't speak to Frank until evening. Frank, fortunately, has not asked, "Spoken to Erna yet?" because he and I are discussing my Uncle Will. "Will is going to have a coronary by-pass on Tuesday. He failed his stress test, failed his angiography, so it's Tuesday."

"That makes two." That's a reference to Harry Troutman, a partner of Papa's who had a coronary by-pass last Wednesday at SouthWest Florida Regional Heart Center and has been slow to recover. "Harry is out of intensive care, but . . ."

"O.K., Edith, tell me."

"Harry has developed a pneumonia. Mama spoke to Doris Troutman—you remember Doris: She was at our wedding. Doris is very upset with the doctors, couldn't find her cardiologist over New Year's."

"Doesn't say much for modern medicine in Florida."

"Do you think it's better in Chicago at Rush Memorial?"

"Should be, Edith. It's a University Medical Center."

"That's what I have been telling Dad, 'Move to Chicago. The doctors are better.' You know Dad, I always get the same answer, 'I am not into doctoring. When I get on that assembly line, I'll call you.' "

"How is Dad?"

"I think his arthritis is worse, seems to be affecting his hands now. He is dropping things."

"Don't go playing doctor, Edith."

"I'm going to talk to Mom."

"Edith, quit worrying."

"Who else is going to do it? Erna, Emma?"

"Your mother is a very competent lady."

"Mom said Dad wasn't feeling well."

"Edith, quit worrying."

After the telephone calls to Uncle Will in California, to Doris Troutman in Sarasota, Mama decides, "What this family needs to do is go out to dinner."

"How about Bob Evans?" My dad is into down home cooking, cornbread, biscuits without gravy, eggs and grits, a residual of his army career spent in the South.

"That's off the island, Dad. Why don't we go to the Hilton?"

"Ashamed to be seen entering a fast food restaurant, Mrs. Vevers?" *Mrs. Vevers* is Dad's put-down to Erna.

"No, Dad, I like wine with dinner. Anyway, there is more choice at the Hilton."

Mama, the peace-maker: "I'll make reservations at the Hilton." She smiles at Dad.

"Four at six p.m. See, in time for the early bird special. You save ten dollars."

"Just don't forget, no one orders espresso. I'm not paying $2.75 for a cup of espresso."

"O.K., Robert, I'll make you your espresso when we get back."

At dinner it is Erna who ordered Chardonnay. She tastes, the chilled wine. "Fine." As we are served Dad supplies his connoisseurship. "Too sweet, too soft."

"Now you are a wine maven." This from Erna.

"Leave your dad alone. He knows," Mama defended.

The bill is placed in the center of the table. It is Dad who picks it up.

The television goes on as soon as we get through the cottage door. Images of troops, tanks, aircraft, bomb loading and President Bush's latest statement to the news media. It's then that I get Dad's short version, "You talk war, you get war. I don't like to see the service families complaining on TV, complaining about their husbands being in Saudi Arabia. It's a volunteer army. What did they expect? You takes the pay, you have to expect to play. War is not a game. It's about killing."

"Robert, your espresso."

Demitasse in hand, Papa sits down beside me. "I spoke to Hollings today. He wants to borrow the Bombergs."

"Papa, the paintings are yours and Mama's do with them as you wish."

"It's only a loan, for exhibition only." Mama hears Papa talking to me. Erna is next door at the guest cottage, no doubt telephoning Leroy Carlson. "Robert, tell Edith the entire story."

"The museum would like to buy the Bombergs."

"All of them?"

"I haven't explored. I just wanted you to know, in case."

"Don't talk about death to me. Don't talk to me about dying." In perfect control without sounding irritated. My achievement.

"Edith, if I can't get the insurance, you will need cash for the taxes. The Bombergs are cash."

"There you go again, talking about death."

"Death and taxes, no avoiding them."

"I know, Dad, I get your business bulletins."

As I look back to last January, did my mother know that her cottages on the Gulf shore were being considered for sale? Each year Mama told me, "Edith, I never thought I would ever have something I always wanted, a cottage with a sea view." On the living room wall behind the sofa, by the secretary, are the Picasso posters Mom carried from Barcelona, had framed in Rock City, wrapped in sheets, comforters, stacked in the Lincoln's trunk to hang in Florida. Their king size bed, the new dishwasher, new refrigerator. Did Mama know? How could Mama give up watching the swallows bathing in the sand under the cape honeysuckle, the pool heated to 84 to 86 degrees? "The only exercise left for us." The neighbors Mama invited for brownies and tea when she wanted Papa to quit working. Mama, a fifty percent partner of Kramer Companies, did know.

"Mama, what do you think of the selling a couple of the Bombergs? It would free up cash."

"It's up to your dad. The Bombergs are his thing."

"Mama—?"

"How is Frank?" Now Mama is doing it, changing subjects.

"Mama, about Leroy Carlson wanting to buy both cottages..."

Mama was out of the rattan sofa and is seated in her armchair with the view of the Gulf, across from me in the rocker, the rocker Dad dismantled in Rock City and reassembled in the cottage.

"Erna wants me to listen to Carlson. Dad thinks we ought to have a talk with him when Emma comes."

"Erna seems very anxious to sell" — now, discretely, circumspectly — "to get a larger distribution."

"You know Erna, always planning. That's the way she is like your dad, always searching for better opportunities."

"Erna mentioned going to France."

"You ask her, Edith. To me Erna has only spoken of how much better off we, your dad and I, would be in a condo."

"On the fourth floor, away from the surf, the beach?"

"Erna is talking about maintenance, security elevators. The view would be the same."

Mama knew, Papa knew, Erna knew. Edith would be informed and left with the details, attorneys, contracts, abstracts, transfers, distributions, taking care of Mom and Dad, and assuring Erna and Emma, "Your check is in the mail."

"Edith, couldn't we get our check before April 15? Taxes you know."

"No distributions without yearend audits. I'll speak to the auditors as soon I get the yearend."

"Don't worry, you will see your dad will be very cautious with Carlson Construction."

"Mama, there are projects that started last year, four hundred feet east of here. The only thing they have put up is a For Sale sign."

"That is single family and not on the gulf."

My mother knew. A woman who owned two cottages, who received "Please call me if you wish to sell" letters from four realtors every November should know. O.K., Mom and Dad are big kids. Not to worry, Edith. Tomorrow I question my dear Dad, then Erna. I'm making lists. I am like my dad.

At six-thirty a.m. the sliding doors are open to the predawn dark. My dad is on the living room floor, twenty sit-ups, fifteen pelvic thrusts, on to the porch with his pillow on the glass table top, one foot stretched back to the count of twenty then the other, twenty times, next knee bends, ten, twenty leg stretches, finger tips to floor, once, twice. Mom is in the kitchen drinking coffee. "It stops my morning headache."

Dad is on the porch facing the roseate rising sun ascending the waters between Vanderbilt Beach and Marco Island. In the west sky, solid banks of grey. In the east the sun has broken through the morning haze to reflect off the Gulf waters. Dad puts on his sunglasses. His green baseball cap, with the long green bill, "Tree Farm" embroidered in white, worn square—a military style, is pulled down to protect his eyes. "The State Forester gave it to me, Edith, when we signed the farm up for reforestation."

Dad is praying. The morning service "Shachris" reading from the Prayer Book, abridged for Jews in the Armed Forces of the United States. On the khaki cover JWB (Jewish Welfare Board) in a Star of David.

Blessed art thou our Lord, our God, Ruler of the universe. Thou removest sleep from our eyes, yes, slumber from our eyelids.

Dad's are very abridged prayers, selecting what he wishes, passing over the others, but he does stay with the order of prayer. *One generation shall laud thy works to another and shall declare thy mighty acts. They shall utter the fame of thy great goodness.* Dad rises for the the silent devotion, remains standing for the final prayer. *My God, guard my tongue from evil and my lips from speaking deceit, and all who rise up against me for evil may speedily see their design as naught, their purposes defeated. It is for us to praise the Lord of all, to acclaim the might of the God of Creation.* Dad folds the prayer book, returns it the bottom drawer of the dining room buffet to rest until tomorrow morning alongside the Sabbath candles.

"Up early, Edith."

"I wanted to see the sunrise."

"Sunrise at seven-twelve."

"Still praying?"

"Every morning."

"Three times a day is required."

"Sometimes I do twice a day. Sometimes three times, reduced to two or three lines when I have a special appeal."

"Like?"

"Trying to stop the war and if not, getting ready for when things get worse. Have to be prepared. Building my reserves of hope."

"You are fortunate you can pray."

"I learned. I had lots of time to learn."

"Do you really believe in prayer, after what you have been through."

"Without prayer there is nothing. Man can't live without hope."

Edith, ask a direct question. There is nothing to be afraid of. Your father loves you. He respects your judgment. He trusts you to manage and carry on.

Dad's breakfast, half grapefruit, skim milk, and Grape-Nuts. I pour coffee into two cups, half a cup for Dad, a full cup for myself. Mom has gone to dress. Erma won't appear until nine or ten.

"Dad, Erna has been talking about moving to France."

"You know Erna, very entrepreneurial. Couldn't stay in one job. In one year she wanted to be a V.P., in two years the C.E.O. Erna has an idea she wants to open an art gallery in Paris."

Paris in the springtime, horse chestnuts in bloom, lovers on the Seine.

"A gallery?"

"She is looking for gallery space in the Marais."

"What about Michael's Nouvelle Cuisine."

"I guess Michael would stay in San Francisco until . . .

until he sells or leases. He is not going to give up his sweetheart lease."

"Erna have a business plan?"

"Yes, indeed. You know Erna."

"With your money or hers?"

"I guess you would say it's Mama's, if she sells the cottages."

"What if that is insufficient?"

"I asked Erna that."

Dad has finished, gets up, clears the breakfast dishes. "Come, Edith, we'll sit on the porch. I can't stand being indoors."

We had been sitting at the dining room table, the sliding doors to the porch open. I could hear the surf, see the pelicans and plovers, the gulls soaring over the surf, circling and returning to their territorial beach. It can't be eight feet from where we are sitting to table and plastic armchair on the porch.

When I was eight Dad had come home from Korea. *Quiet, Edith, Dad is sleeping*. Dad slept fully dressed, shoes and field jacket, in the gazebo or on a plastic cot under the oaks covered by khaki blankets. Once when Dad was home on leave—I was only six—I had tied Dad to the dining room chair. He and Mom had friends in. They were sitting around the dining room table talking. "How long will the war last in Korea?"

"Quite normal, Mrs. Taylor. You didn't want to lose your father. Your father had come home, you were afraid he would go away again, leave you."

In twenty years and six months, Mom and Dad will be gone. The actuarial report from the insurance company. In twenty years I'll be sixty-six, a woman of a certain age, a woman of means,

and if there are no grandchildren, Dad's estate will go

to Jewish Federation of Charities, colleges, libraries. Not enough dollars to get a room named "The Kramer Memorial," but enough for me to get invitations for hamburgers with the college presidents. Plaques and onyx paperweights with the college's name embossed. Only one answer, Edith: Early retirement. Do something for yourself before you have to start living for Mom and Dad and Erna and Emma. *Let Edith do it.*

The cottages represent ten percent of Mom's and Dad's estate. Diversify your investments. Lose on the stock market, make it up in Art Market. Selling the Bombergs to gain cash would certainly be equal to buying equivalent dollar coverage by paying insurance premiums. Make a note: Investigate equivalent return verses cost of insurance premium.

"Making progress with Carlson?"

"Charming man, Edith."

"They all are when they want something."

"Very young to be running a development company."

"How old is he?"

"Less than forty."

"That's not young anymore. Our bank president is only thirty-eight."

"How old when you and Mama when you started bulding?"

"More than forty, but there was a war in 1950."

Papa never says *Korea*, never says *prisoner of war*, never says *Veterans Hospital*, Mama told me.

"Your dad had a difficult time in a place where it wasn't easy for him."

"Edith, would you like to meet Mr. Carlson. I could have him come over this afternoon."

"I would like that, Papa."

"You really should meet him. You may be doing business with him over the years."

I almost said, "Don't talk about death to me, Papa. I can't stand it." It's bad enough filing your notes due in 1996 with addendums, "if Mom and I are gone." Gift taxes to be filed in 1991 for transfers of property in 2001.

"Papa, you can't set up a GRIT trust in anticipation of death." Papa knows a ten year transfer gives him the greatest tax benefit, and should he or Mama die, the cost of setting up the trust, everything, would be lost. Papa and Mama will live for at least ten years to use up their losses on their annual joint tax return. That's why Papa is always planning, talks of buying insurance; he is sure he will not die.

"That's how Dad came home to you and me, Edith. He knew he was going to walk out of that p.o.w. camp alive and come home to us. One day you will understand, Edith; it's because he was in a cell. That's why Papa can't stand being indoors."

Dad has dialed. "Leroy at two p.m.," Dad writes in his journal, shuts it. "Enough. Edith, you want to go swimming? Millie, you want to go swimming?"

"I was waiting breakfast for Erna."

"Erna is a big girl."

The pool, heated in full sun, protected from the birds by a total screen. "I don't know what I would do without a pool."

Nobody is selling yet, Mama.

Mom swims on her back. Dad crawls, breast strokes, underwater for ten minutes, then takes off his goggles, begins his exercises, ten leg lifts, then five right knee to jaw, left knee to jaw: impossible to him. There is a gap of twenty inches. "That's the hip that was injured." Beatings across the lower back on Papa's hips over the hip joint. The scars are faint broad white streaks. Dad replaces his T-shirt as soon as he is out of the pool. Dad never goes without a shirt. If his swim trunks slips below his left hip, he stops swimming, pulls it up. The left hip that is caved, hollowed out, makes him walk like the sheriff hero of a black and white Saturday afternoon cowboy serial, swaying from side to side. "Once your papa was tall and straight like in our wedding picture." Tall and straight in his summer uniform and hat square, eyes front: twenty-one and Mama only twenty before scoliosis, degeneration of the spine, before Papa was in the Veterans Hospital.

"Mama, what's for lunch?"

"A whole frig full."

"I'm hungry."

"You should eat breakfast, Edith."

"Yes, Papa. Papa, I was talking to Mother."

I did not tell Papa, "Erna's getting a divorce. Erna got the house. Erna has one hundred and sixty thousand dollars in the Sanibel Island Bank. Erna received one hundred thousand dollars in a cash settlement from Michael. Erna has enough; I have enough, Papa."

I went in for lunch.

Chapter 7

Edith

Leroy Carlson is an "upmarket" developer. "Yes, Mr. Kramer, Mrs. Kramer, Mrs. Taylor, Mrs. Vevers.

"With your view of the Gulf, we are planning an upmarket development. Only ten or twelve owners who will have all the amenities of a fine hotel, newspapers delivered seven days a week, rental service for those owners who wish it. Rental not for a week or two, but at least for a month, and a resale service. We are considering a no-fee resale service as a pre-construction buying incentive."

The agent's fee will be hidden by an increase in the closing costs.

Forty years old, a yuppie dressed in Ralph Lauren's "Polo." That's one thing Papa is right about: Everyone is clever in an upmarket. Rising real estate prices bail out poorly planned, overfinanced or overleveraged projects.

Edith, don't tell Papa, "Be careful."

Leroy Carlson: casual blue golf shirt, the white baggy Ralph Lauren cut trousers: the emblems of success. That and the Mercedes, or is it the Jaguar this year? Blond from the sun, confident from success. All leather attaché case on the floor beside his armchair. Dad has placed Carlson in the armchair with the view of the Gulf. The sun is in Leroy's eyes. He reaches into the case. Black frames, black lens sun glasses, the *a la mode* 1960's vintage look.

Carlson's wristwatch, Ebel like Erna's, not one of those uncouth Rolex wearers. Ebel gold and platinum, six thousand dollars of non-glare elegance, of opulent good taste.

Good old Papa, always directly to business. "The cottages are Mrs. Kramer's."

"I know that. Mrs. Kramer, I am sure that you will find the condominiums we build all that you could ever hope in the way of appliances and furnishings."

Leroy Carlson, marketing corporation. Mama's expression hasn't changed; she sits to the left of Leroy Carlson.

Carlson could be older. He may have had a face job to make him look thin, fit. Papa looked like that twenty years ago. Papa, who in order to control his pain ("It's worse in the afternoons after I sit."), had to swim. Papa was fit. Leroy keeps fit at his health club.

Carlson's competitive edge, fitness, diet, a gold wedding ring on his left hand. Is he married to his second trophy wife? With whom he plays mixed doubles tennis, or has she already gone back to S.F.W. to take university courses to finish her M.B.A., or are they skimming from their limited partners through self-dealing fees, a house painting company owned by Mrs. Leroy Carlson or a landscape maintenance contract to L & C. Taking eighteen percent up front from their investors for putting the deal together. Carlson gets the upfront million, goes bankrupt, Mama loses her cottages.

Papa: "Have you pre-sold any of the condos?"

"Difficult, Mr. Kramer. It's difficult for prospective owners to visualize. We will finish one building and then of course we hope to have the condos sold before we put up the second or third building."

Papa: "How are you going to finance the construction loan?"

Papa stops. "That is, until you sell your condos."

"Limited partners as investors."

Doctors, lawyers, orthodontists, chiropractors, chiropodists, television actors looking for growth and write-offs. "With interim financing in place, we could begin construction this fall."

"So soon."

"Once we control the land, we can, with your permission, of course, Mrs. Kramer."

Mama, don't subordinate. You wait until all the condos are sold until you get paid. Carlson will get years of free use of your money.

Nicely now, Edith.

"I hope you don't expect my mother to wait for her sale proceeds."

Leroy turns towards me. I am sitting behind Papa in the shade. Erna is beside Mama to whisper her approval.

It's just the way we sat down, Edith, nothing more.

"Mrs. Kramer would have to wait for her condo to be completed anyway." I mark down, *Mama gets condo in first building to be completed.*

Papa: "If you fail to get the private investors . . .?"

Leroy is ready for that one. "Mr. Morris at the Southwest Regional Bank in Saint Petersburg has offered us financing."

I mark down, *Check interest rate, length of commitment, amount of commitment.* "Have you had other loans with Southwest?"

"This would be our second, Mrs. Taylor." I write down, *Visit Morris, loan officer.* "There are advantages to building in a soft market."

"It is more difficult to get financing."

"Perhaps in the north, Mrs. Taylor. Mr. Morris has assured me . . ."

Payoffs, upfront fees to loan officers for loans that will never be repaid. Mama's land tied up in years of litigation.

"No advances, Mrs. Taylor, to any of the contractors until you receive the quit claims, the architect's release, and, Mrs. Taylor, we expect you to visit the site. On-site visits is where you learn to assess the progress of the job. We like to have our payouts stay at least ten percent behind the job. Not ahead of the job."

In twenty-two years, M.B.A. loan officer to economics research manager.

"If there are no more questions, we can talk about the price."

"About the heated pool—" It's Mama.

"We will make every effort to leave the pool exactly where it is." Leroy Carlson was waiting for that. He reaches into attaché case. "An architectural rendering in three colors. You name it, you got it—fantasy on paper for brochures that promise 'Live on a tropical island, invest in this sun-drenched coast close to the regional medical center.'

"In this rendering, you can't see the pool, Mrs. Kramer, but it's behind our three buildings. Each building will be situated to have a view of the gulf."

"I do hope Mom and Dad will not have to walk across a parking lot to use the pool."

"The architectural drawings are in a very preliminary stage."

I write down, *Review and approve pool location.*

"Mrs. Kramer, I talked to Mrs. Vevers about the price, three hundred thousand when you sign the sales contract."

"And Mom and Dad get a condo worth more than

three hundred thousand to live in. A like exchange, Dad. You cut your taxes in half." Erna's pleading.

Mama says nothing. Papa says nothing.

"You could live in the cottages until construction begins." An assurance from Leroy Carlson.

I write down *Define rents to be paid during construction*.

Mama says nothing. Papa says nothing.

"The condo would be fully furnished." Assurance number two. .The Carlson Companies have a furniture subsidiary selling at retail to Carlson Marketing Corporation, delivered by Carlson Trucking Corporation . . .Carlson is too anxious.

Mama: "I like my own furniture."

"No problem at all, Mama, Mr. Carlson will move your furniture for you." Assurance number three from Erna.

Erna is picking up an origination fee. Erna brought the sale of the cottages to Carlson for a three percent upfront fee. On six hundred thousand, another eighteen thousand for her Gallery. Erna in the regentrified Marais, close to the Pompidou and just around the corner from the Picasso museum. The Marais will be like Soho in 1980, a center for trendy, American contemporary art. The rendering is back in the case, Papa has gotten up, Leroy gets up, straightens his beeper. "I could meet with you again, whenever you wish." Assurance number four.

Papa: "I'll call you."

Erna: "We will keep in touch."

"Would you like to have lunch with me, visit some of our other projects see the kind of work we do?" This addressed to Mama and Papa, now standing together at the porch door.

Papa: "I'm sorry, I don't do lunch."

Mama: "Mr. Kramer swims every noon, has for years and years."

"Perhaps I could call for you some afternoon?"

Papa: "Any day but Thursday. Thursday is my at-home business day.

"What business were you in, Mr. Kramer?"

"Real estate, Mr. Carlson."

"I'm sorry, I forgot. Mrs. Vevers did mention it to me. Mrs. Vevers has told me of your successes."

With Dad, that is a no-no. A *faux pas*, a misstep, more than a glitch; for him that is not flattery. To him that is invasion of privacy.

"Edith, no credit reports to Dun and Bradstreet, no credit reports to anyone on the telephone. We don't talk about money, yours or mine, or the family's, in public, where strangers are present. That kind of talk is only within the family."

"We had an upmarket for a long time . . ." Dad doesn't finish.

Carlson hasn't heard him. He is out the porch door; on the walk he turns. "Can I call you, by the fifteenth?"

"We will call you, Mr. Carlson." That's Mama.

Papa, bent forward, has walked into the kitchen. It's time for his pill before he and Mama hand in hand go for their beach walk into the sunset. Thursday night is pizza, cheese and mushroom for us and one quarter of anchovy for Mama. "I'm sorry, Dad, no dark beer."

"Florida is a lite beer state, full of light and hope."

"What did you say, Robert?" Mama is in the kitchen making the salad.

Dad is seated at the dining room table watching *McNeal-Lehrer*. "Looks like another war, Millie."

Erna comes in with the pizza. "Got you ten percent off, Papa, used your local resident's coupon."

"Ten percent is ten percent. How much are you getting on your reserves, Erna?"

In the vault will be Papa's instructions, the records of any extra distributions in 1984, 1985, 1986, 1987, 1988, 1989, 1990, the record of all the distributions.

See if gift tax reports were filed or were there just signed notes that if Erna found she could destroy. "Dearest Edith, you have the only key to the vault . . . Edith, Erna needs you." Emmie doesn't care. *Mrs. Taylor, you have this excessive need to be needed.* It's not excessive. Erna and Emmie are in San Francisco. Emmie . . . Emmie isn't ready for meetings, allocations, distributions. Emmie is still into causes. "Save the Whales" . . ."Feed the Starving Children in Ethiopia." Afro-Americans, Hispanics. It's lucky she married a man who can cook. Poor Doctor Bernie Schwartz.

We Kramer girls are all good eaters. On me it's beginning to show. I think Emmie will get fat when she begins to sit down to eat.

After supper Papa is reading Updike, *Rabbit at Rest*. Mama was in the crossword, Erna and I are clearing. "Seems like more than a fair deal for Mama."

"Only if she wants it, Erna."

"It's one of those deals where everyone could benefit."

"Sounds too good to be true."

"Mama gets the same view, Papa doesn't care where he is if he can swim, walk the beach and read."

"Erna, tell me, how are we all going to be together in a condo?"

"I didn't think you cared. I thought you only came because you didn't want to hurt Mama by refusing."

"No. I want to be with you and Emmy."

"You get enough of Mama and Papa all year long. Why don't you admit it?"

"Who else is going to do it?"

"That's not what I asked you."

"You want some espresso, Erna? I'm making some for Dad."

"Not that dehydrated powdered stuff. I don't know how Dad can drink that dishwater."

Chapter 8

Edith

Erna is not my idea of a penitent, standing up with the congregation, beating her breast on the first Yom Kippur after

Mama died for the sins of omissions, for the sins of commission. *Lord, forgive* . . .But there is Erna, my own sister, who I took care of since the day Mama brought her home from the Rock City Public Hospital, standing in front of the Rock City congregation, loudly reciting the Kaddish, the memorial prayers, for Mama. Making up for how she spoke in front of Mama? Didn't she realize what that did to Papa?

Maybe it's all Papa's fault; maybe he could have spoken to Erna, "That is no way to talk to your mother." It may have stopped Erna, maybe not. Erna was born angry. Something to do with bonding, not bonding with her mother during those first early months. Papa was gone, Mama all alone. I was in kindergarten. Mama had all day with Erna. I helped Mama. I changed Erna. That first year Papa came home I remember I was eight. Mama insisting, "Papa is fine."

"Mama, why does Papa stay by himself on the porch? Mama, why doesn't Papa play with me?"

All Papa had to say to Erna the first time she attacked him and Mama was, "Erna, why do you hate me so? What have I done to you?"

At least he could have said, "Did you hear what you said, how you spoke to us? Do you realize what you have done to your mother? Look at your mother. Your mother hasn't slept in days. She spends her nights writing letters to you. Pleading letters, imploring letters."

I found this one in the handbag Mama had with her when she died.

> Dear Erna:
> Please don't speak to your dad that way. Whatever he did to you doesn't deserve the kind of anger you vent on him. Your dad did the best he could. We both made mistakes in raising you. When you have children you will find that you too will make mistakes. I do hope that your children will never speak to you as you have to us. For your father's sake, please do try to control your temper. Your mother and father love you, and in our way we did the best we could.
> Your mother,
> M.

Mom never mailed that letter; it was sealed, addressed, stamped, ready. Mama was waiting until Erna would get her life together, get over the trauma of her divorce. I should have mailed the letter. I didn't because I don't know how to handle Erna, how to please her. Mama and Papa were the ones Erna should have tried to please, or at least not to hurt. It doesn't take all that much effort to say "Good morning, Dad." Dad smiles, "Good morning, Edith, sleep well?"

Erna did so many little things to hurt Dad on purpose. Erna is spiteful; she wouldn't even take a painting from Dad's collection. He would have given her anything she liked. "The Chase is too big. Who wants fish and a copper pot in their home? . . . Nordfeldt's 1940 landscapes are too stark. Anyway, Marsden Hartley did it better." Erna knows art. That's what so perverse. Dad wanted to share, to give. Erna wouldn't take. "I'm going to make it on my own, Edith."

"No one makes on their own, Erna, not these days. Look at yourself, all the advantages Dad and Mom gave you."

"They should have let me struggle more. I would have achieved more on my own."

Perverse, that's what Erna's thinking is, plainly contrary and capricious.

Now she is sorry, running to services to pray for her dead mother.

"You O.K., Dad?"

"I'm O.K., Edith."

"Erna saying anything to you?"

"About what?"

"About anything."

"Erna said she wasn't going to stop in Rock City on her way to Paris."

"Erna invite you to Paris, Papa?"

Papa didn't answer. Papa protecting Erna from her big sister.

It was our first Passover Seder without Mama. Dad tries to help me when he comes to visit. He had put out the placemats, the crystal. Before supper in Rock City Dad used to sit on the counter, on the far side of the sink, watched Mama peeling carrots. Then he would get behind Mama, kiss her on the neck.

"Robert, you only kiss me when I am working."

I was at the counter; Dad stood beside me, leaned back to take the weight off his spine. Dad hadn't answered to *Erna invite you to Paris?*

"Did Erna invite you?" I say again.

"I'm sure she will."

Dad sat on the chair beside me. Ours is an island kitchen, without counters to sit on.

"I wait for Mama to call me. Mama used to call me every Tuesday morning before she went to her bookclub."

"I miss Mama."

"I know you do, Papa. I do too, Papa, just for girl talk. On a Friday afternoon if I wanted for fix something special for Shabbus I would call up Mama just to talk, 'to get your recipe for kugel, Mama.'"

"You can have Mama's cookbooks."

"What are you going to do with the house, Papa? All alone in that big house?"

"I have good neighbors."

"Papa, thanks for the money."

"Mama left it for you."

"I can't thank Mama."

"We thank with deeds of loving kindness, for the living and the dead."

"Papa, you going to the *minyan*?"

"Every morning, Monday to Friday."

"Why don't you go on Saturday and Sunday? It would get you out of the house. Go out to breakfast with the boys."

"On Saturday and Sunday I was alone with Mama, just she and I. I sat in my chair, looked at Mama, looked at the paintings, read. Once Mama hung a painting, she never moved it." Papa chuckled. "That is unless I bought a bigger one. Then Mama moved the paintings from my den to make room, but in the living room in the dining room, it's all like it was for years."

The Picabia on the wall behind the spiral staircase. In the living room the Chase between the two north windows, sculptured beige shades on the window wall. Light, airy, twenty-two foot ceiling because Dad, "Dad doesn't like curtains, Dad feels space differently than you and I, Edith. Dad is more comfortable when he has more light around him."

"Is that why Dad used to stay in the gazebo?"

"Dad, you want to come to live with Frank and me?"

"Not yet, Edith, not yet."

"You could have your own room. You wouldn't have to cook."

"I don't cook now, Edith. You want me to help you?"

"Sure, Papa, put the ice in the pitcher."

Papa read the Passover *Hagaddah*. I had prepared the Seder, the *matza*, the *charses*, the bitter herbs, the shank bone, the Kosher for Passover wine. Papa noticed.

"You done good, Edith. Done real good." When Papa is pleased, he talks down home Southern. "Where did you learn to talk like that, Dad?"

"Had a lot of boys from southern Tennessee in my company."

Papa didn't put his arms around me nor kiss me. Mama was the only one he ever put his arms around. Dad must be afraid of his daughters, afraid of their rejection. I don't put my arms around my dad. I don't hug him or kiss him. Dad kisses me on my forehead. Ridiculous, isn't it. That's how it is. How that distance happened, how it all began, in a warm loving Jewish family. How did all that distance come between us? Why can't we hug and kiss?

I tried it after the Seder. Dad was "helping," clearing the dishes. He had put the dishes in the sink. I put my arms around him. "I love you, Papa."

When I said that, Papa answered, "Thanks."

Why would he thank me for kissing him?

That's how the year went. Mom was gone and life continued.

I made the Seder; Bernie and Emmie came for the second night. Erna . . .I think Erna just couldn't face Papa.

"Papa, I have to get the house sold; I can't take off. Why don't you come out here? It will do you good."

Book III

Chapter 9

Erna

We buried Mama on the Iowa Knoll. Snow and cold and the west wind. In the family plot on this mound on the Mississippi bluff with the headstone of black marble on which the letters are fading, but the message is distinct:
SEEK JUSTICE, LOVE MERCY.
WALK HUMBLY WITH THY GOD.
MICAH.

At the graveside we, her daughters, cried and shoveled the frozen soil onto Mama's wooden coffin. Papa did not cry. He just stood, his face to the wind. We recited the Kaddish: *Magnified and sanctified be the great home of God throughout the world which He hath created according to his will. May He who establisheth peace in the heavens grant peace unto us and unto all Israel and say Amen.*

The faces at the Meal of Consolation were mostly old, with red eyes, women of a certain age many already widowed, living independent lives, praying not to become a burden to their children in California or Chicago or Texas.

The rabbi had honored my mama's request that he not use his "woman of virtue" speech. Instead he spoke of Mildred Kramer's charities, and of her raising three daughters. He made no mention of my dad, of their life together. I am sure I know why. Dad must have told the rabbi, "The old are more used to death. Try to console our daughters."

During the week of Shiva callers came from the congregation, from Mama's charities and book study, and always the neighbors with food. "You don't know me, but your mother was so proud of her daughters. She never bragged much, but now and then she told me about you."

"Your mother was my support system."

"Your mother was a good woman. Never said no to me."

"Your mother did book reviews that were truly scholarly. That is not why I am here. I wanted to tell you what she did for our community."

"Whatever we needed, and when we needed a bit of shaking up to do better. your mom was there with direction. You might say that your mother added direction to the YWCA Board."

"Most of what your mother did she did anonymously. We on the board of course knew, that was the way she wanted it."

The visitors came and went, and Papa just sat in his chair, dazed. From time to time he turned the chair to look at the back yard, at the oaks. "Those trees are about one hundred and sixty years old."

The *minyan* met at our home for the morning prayers.

Blessed are thou, O Lord our God, King of the Universe, who raisest up those who are bowed down. Blessed art thou, O Lord our God, King of the Universe, who givest strength to the weary.

I tried prayer; it didn't help, but I couldn't tell that to Papa. On the Saturday during the Shiva we went to services, myself. There were my same doubts about God. "Your strength comes from God," said the rabbi in his sermon.

"It will be better. Hope for a better tomorrow. Without hope there is no life for anyone." That is what my dad answered when I asked, "You O.K.?"

I had heard my mother in her doubts. "I don't have your faith, Bob." I heard my mother in her anger with Papa. "You can do better, Bob." My dad never answered.

"Bob, why didn't you consult me?"

"I was trying to protect you."

Then my mother louder, louder. "That is arrogant behavior, Bob. I don't do a thing without telling you, without asking you, and I have to find out what you did from others."

"It's not a sin, Millie. I didn't want to get you involved."

"I'm not going along with that, Bob."

"I haven't done it yet. I felt boxed in, so I threatened to do it."

"It's that everyone in town knows what you said."

"I was only trying to protect you."

Dad . . .Well, Dad couldn't handle Mom, not when she went on her "my rights" things.

Dad's explanation, "I never intended to hurt you, Millie . . . Millie, I had no motive. I said nothing that I thought could hurt you."

"You didn't consult with me."

"You didn't ask me."

"You are correct, Millie. I should have."

That argument was about a funeral. Dad threatened to join the Reformed Temple because they allowed funerals from their synagogue, and Mama said, "You go."

"I just didn't want to be buried from a parlor," was my dad's last words to Mama, but he lost the argument. Mama was buried from a parlor. Dad has yet to go "reform."

That was the last big argument I heard. That was thirty years ago. Mama had her rights.

I have mine.

Erna, your language is inappropriate, for a woman with your education. Fuck is not a word one uses in conversation. I saw that in Mama's face: fuck is inappropriate at the Kramers.

"That man is a shit." Dad was relating his relationship with a tenant who wished to lease space from him.

"Bob, a man of your education can surely find a better word in your vocabulary."

"Millie, I got angry."

"Bob, that only demeans you."

"Millie, he went to the mayor, complained about me to the mayor."

"That language only demeans you." Dad didn't say anything, but then he turned to Mom. "I could have called him worse. I learned worse in the cavalry."

"Bob, you are seventy years old."

That's what Dad and Mother's arguments were about. I envied her, her arguments. With Michael I couldn't argue. Michael was more the "European" husband, the □patron□, than my dad who was born in Sczucyn, Poland. I have had it with men who want to "protect me" for my own good. Erna Kramer, with what you know and your papa's money, you can make it.

"I don't need advice on how to."

Dad gave me a prayer book to take with me. "We have much to be thankful for, Erna."

"Yes, Papa."

Papa retreats into his prayer book. Emmie retreats into her good deeds, Edith . . .Edith into her support network of girlfriends, with miserable jobs they chose for themselves, husbands that step out on them, children with "problems."

I see it. I am the most like Mama and Papa. I am going to make it—if not on my own exactly, but with my own efforts.

I remember when I was growing up Papa was angry, Mama was angry. Maybe over different things than what makes me angry. Papa made good, they did good; so in time and with success, they became less angry. With age I too will be less angry.

"How are you doing, Erna?"

"Doing the best I can, Papa."

"Your mother always thought I could do better."

"Could you have, Papa?"

"I surely tried."

"Maybe Mama's standards were too high."

"I never dared tell her that."

"You have faith, Papa."

"Mama kept looking for hers."

"Do you think Mama found her faith?'

"When?"

"In that second when Mama saw the truck coming, going to crush her."

"I don't know, Erna. I don't know."

Chapter 10

Erna

Mama was not difficult to talk to. What was difficult was to find her alone, away from her self-appointed tasks. Up at six a.m., she read her novels, then made the coffee, did the housework, out to the grocery, to the fish market with a handful of coupons. She always came home with pink or red gladioli whose stems she cut off with her carving knife. Before lunch she and Dad went swimming. The lunch dishes were in the dishwasher, and Mama into *The New York Times'* crossword puzzle. I see it even now: Mama is on the porch; Dad is writing. I have to wait until Dad goes downtown to get the mail to speak to Mama. Mama is dozing in the lounge chair; Edith is on the beach writing in her portfolio, exhortations to her staff: "Be sure the economics forecasts get to the printer," exorcising her guilts on lined yellow legal paper to her counselor, a catharsis via the mail to maintain their relationship so that Edith won't waiver from gaining insights, revelations of self while she is enjoying Sanibel.

Edith writes to her counselor, "It would be so nice if we could have dinner." The counselor no doubt is a latent lesbian, a threat to Edith and Frank's happy marriage, twenty-five years of childless bliss on the North Shore.

Knowing Edith, she is still working out why and what happened fifteen years ago.

"That's all there is, Edith. The shrinks can pull you apart, they can't put you together. That you do yourself. I learned that in eighteen months."

On the lounge, Mama has roused herself, is stretching.

"Mama?"

"Yes, Erna."

"Edith told me about Dad dropping things. It doesn't look too bad to me."

"Not yet, but, anyway, it could never happen . . . but then it could."

"Don't be so damn mysterious. What are you talking about?"

"I wrote to you. Papa's spinal nerves are damaged. It's the inflammation. That is what is interfering with his function."

"Dad walks pretty well."

"He is in greater pain than ever. I wrote to you about it."

"I guess I have had other things on my mind."

"Your job?"

"No, packaging mortgages is no big strain on my intellect."

"The restaurant?"

"I have been going through . . . you know . . . Whither am I drifting. To hell with the restaurant. What I am going to do with the rest of my life."

"We all do that before our fortieth birthday. That is, everybody I know did that but your father. He was too busy to notice, and suddenly we are almost seventy, and he doesn't even recognize that. What do you want from Dad, Erna?"

"I want him to quit, get rid of the properties. We don't need it. Edith can take over. All he has to do is ask her. She would do anything for Dad."

"It's not that he doesn't trust Edith, he does. It's just he has never asked anybody to do for him. Never expected any help. The only one he have ever asks for help is the God above."

"Dad still praying every morning?"

"Wake up and watch him. Sunrise at seven-twelve, Dad is facing east, praying. It works for him."

"Sharing his responsibilities would help him more and all of us, too. I'm sorry, Mama, I said too much, but then that's what getting the family together is for. Mama, have you ever told Dad, 'I am quitting, you are quitting.'?"

"I tell, he doesn't hear. Now he may listen. Maybe he was right years ago not to listen to me, to go on from one project to the next, but now we don't need it."

"Mama, my divorce settlement with Michael is all in place, one hundred thousand now, two hundred thousand when he sells the restaurant or in six and a half years, whichever comes first."

"Dad didn't tell me that."

"What did Dad tell you?"

"You were getting divorced. I don't understand why you didn't you walk out sooner? Eight years ago Papa began giving you money. Eight years ago, so you could do anything you wanted."

"No guts, Mama. Took me a long time to get it all together. Michael was a father figure to me. I had to break those ties."

"Your father didn't beat you."

"No, he only neglected me."

"Let's not go into that again. Your father was in a prison camp, then in a Veterans Hospital, and it took time for him to come back to his family."

"He didn't have to be in the army."

"He thought he did."

"He didn't have to get captured."

"He stayed with the wounded."

"Uncle Will told me all about it. 'Boy Hero of the Plains' is what Will calls Dad."

"Will doesn't understand your father."

"You do?"

"Erna, that is not your problem, that is Dad's and mine. You want to talk about yours, I am here. If not, I'll start supper."

That's my folks' generation, no time for talk, no time for delving, exploring, understanding. Mama was almost like Dad, not quite so controlled, but almost. Dad's life is like a campaign. First he determines his goals, what he intends to achieve, and then how he intends to go about it. Then he gets on with it.

"Now you have your MBA, Erna. You are going to work for a company that puts deals together. It's all risk. If you can stand it, do it. If not, don't, find a way out. There is no shame in retreat. Retreat will give you a chance to fight again."

Dad changed fight to try and the lecture stopped. I had heard the story from Uncle Will: "Your dad's company had been retreating for days to keep from being surrounded. The Chinese came in from behind, mined the roads. There were lots of wounded. Anyway, your dad had a way out. He chose to stay."

"Why, Uncle Will?"

"Ask him."

I never have. One day I will.

There I was, finally, face to face with Mama. "Mama, I need the hundred thousand. I need to do something for myself, something I believe in."

"Dad told me. Don't get so passionate. Sit down, tell me about the gallery."

My business plan is ready, my correspondence completed. "I have everything going for me, Mama. I speak

French, I speak English. I have Lester Johnson's and Nathan Olivera's promises to let me represent them."

"They are not new discoveries. They have been around for thirty years."

"Not in France. That's the advantage. Here in the USA they are well known; in France they become discoveries. With the dollar down, the franc up, it's cheaper for the French to buy American."

Mama doesn't say a thing about my wish to give up fringe benefits, medical coverage, paid holidays, regular nine to five hours, no weekends, for working nights, Saturdays, Sundays. Gallery openings and press releases, preparing catalogs, cadging publicity.

"You thought this out. You know what Dad will tell you, 'You had better have a way out before you go in.'"

"You and Dad did it all by yourself. I want to try it, too."

"There were two of us."

"Mama, look at this list: European artists that are willing to go with me. Leonardo Cremonini. The Museum of Modern Art bought his paintings. Co Westerik. He lives in Rotterdam. That's not far from Paris. Derek Boshier. Stuart Brisley. Bernard Cohen. They are in London. Cohen had a showing in Paris at the National Museum of Modern Art."

"That was seventeen years ago, Erna. Who is going to remember Bernard Cohen?"

"That's my job, show and tell, and sell."

"Slogans don't sell paintings."

"These are great painters. If you don't believe in Lester Johnson, why do you keep buying them?"

Mama laughed. Mama hardly ever laughed. Good sign or bad?

"All right, already, all right. You need a hundred thousand dollars, we'll see. I'll talk to Papa."

I started up.

"Where are you going?"

"I thought you wanted to start supper."

"We'll eat spaghetti. With Becks beer, your dad will eat anything. Spaghetti all right with you, Erna?"

"You don't mind if I have some red wine."

"Dad only has the *vin ordinaire*."

"It will have to do," and I laughed.

"Why are you laughing?"

"I was thinking of Michael's. 'The white with the fish, madam; the red with the onion soup, and the sorbet to clean the palate . . . The strawberries dipped in chocolate especially for you . . . The flourless chocolate cake is the house specialty, made in our ovens.' Mama, our cake comes in from a bakery, the sorbet hurts my teeth and the strawberries give me a rash. And Michael's wine is overpriced."

"You sound like your dad. Erna, have you told Edith?"

"Some, Mama, not everything."

"You had better tell Edith. You know how Dad is. First he'll talk to me, then he'll talk to Edith. Then he'll run several alternative plans. He'll try to do the best he can for you. You know that, don't you?"

"I know, Mama."

"Go down, talk to Edith, take her for a walk. She is always working. Erna, don't forget — tell her everything."

Caught again. How to explain *In 1996 I'll have two hundred thousand dollars more*: Sins of omission, sins of commission — both are sins.

I'll begin with, "Mama was pleased that I got rid of the *gruber goy*."

Then Edith will say, "You finally got your act together. If you are pleased, I am pleased. Erna, why didn't you tell me about Michael's note to you? Why can't you tell a straight, complete story with all the facts?"

"My selective omission was to gain your support for sale of the cottages. I can't wait six years, Edith. I am 40 years old." Or, maybe, "Edith, I wasn't thinking."

"That won't do, Erna."

"Edith, I forgot."

"Forgot two hundred thousand dollars due in 1996? You got a note and an assignment, didn't you?"

Down the steps to the beach. Edith turned, saw me coming, immediately shut the leather-covered portfolio, put it inside her "Chicago Art Institute" beach bag.

"Aren't you hot sitting out here?"

"I was just coming in. What is Mama making for supper?"

"Spaghetti. She doesn't need your help."

"I have to set the table."

I looked at my watch. "You have a half hour. We won't eat until *McNeal-Lehrer* goes on."

Edith takes my left hand, draws my wrist watch towards her. "Michael didn't take back the Ebel watch. You are five thousand up."

"I paid for that watch, bought it for myself."

"You lied again, Erna. Still lying, little Erna?"

"Had to save face, protect Michael's reputation for generosity."

"That pig generous?"

"You want to go for a walk, Edie? I want to talk."

We walked west. Edith heavier than ever, trying to cover her thickened thighs and belly with that awful black cover-up. To the bank Edith wears designer work clothes, Perry Ellis, Brooks Brothers; on vacation she dresses like a *bubba*, a grandmother. Edith bends down, picks up piece of coral. It goes into her pocket, she adds an olive shell, stops, shakes the sand from her sandals. "I have to buy beach slippers."

"Wear Mama's. I do. I am waiting for a rainy day to go shopping. I spoke to Dad. You are in his review process. I want to file an amendment. I'll tell Dad myself, or you can tell him."

"Tell Dad what?"

"I'll get two hundred thousand more in '96 from Michael."

Edith stops, turns a piece of driftwood over with her toe, bends down. "Looks like a fish."

"Edith, I am sorry, I forgot."

"Forgot two hundred thousand due in 1996? The note stashed in your vault? The photocopy with your attorney? Erna, why don't you trust me?"

"I do."

"Forget it." Edith looks at her watch, turns back. "Come on, we can help Mama."

"How shall I put it to Dad?"

"Just tell the truth. Try the truth, the first time."

"I didn't lie."

"The whole truth, nothing but the truth."

"Edith, what am I going to tell Dad?

"Tell him the truth."

"I was afraid you wouldn't help me if I told you I'm going to get two hundred thousand in six years. Edith, I am forty years old. I have wasted ten years. I can't wait six years to start my gallery."

"You are just like Dad, Erna. You never learn; you continue to make the same mistakes. Papa thought his partners weren't going to continue to steal from him—that after he caught them once, twice."

"O.K., I'll tell Papa like I explained it to you. It was exactly like that, no guts, afraid I wouldn't get the cottages sold. I am still afraid of failing."

"Who isn't?"

"You don't seem to be."

"Little do you know."

"Edith, will you tell Dad I told you?"

"Sure. Take my advice, Erna. Around here everybody will know anyway. Tell Papa tonight. While we are having dinner, or after *McNeal-Lehrer*. It will be better for you."

Papa was sitting on the porch, in the dark. It was Mama who made sure the porch light wouldn't work so Papa couldn't work at night. Papa sat looking at the moon rise over Ft. Myers Beach, reflect off the surf.

"Sit down, Erna. Pity you don't get up early. You missed it this morning—the full moon was setting while the sun was rising, a regular tropical island. No wonder your mother hates to go back to Rock City."

"You could quit, live here year around."

"Not yet."

"When?"

"When I get some of the real estate sold."

"You have said that for twelve years."

"I haven't turned down any offers."

"You haven't looked for any buyers, either."

"Each spring I test the market. This spring, who can tell? If I get any interest, I'll sell. All right, I promise to put a few lots up for sale."

"A couple of lots at a time, it will take ten years to sell the first subdivision."

"I have plenty of time. I am only sixty-nine, in the spring." Papa is laughing. "Of course, if the Japanese buy me out..."

"What would you do then?"

"Write my autobiography or a business guide, *How to Survive in Real Estate in a Downmarket,* or a play. Or a novel about three daughters who each January come to visit their parents in Florida."

"Then what happens?"

"One gets a divorce."

That was my opening. "And doesn't tell you that she will get two hundred thousand in '96," I finished for Dad.

Dad wasn't upset; he was laughing. "With Michael you may never get paid."

"I have his note."

"He is in France, the restaurant is sold or closed. You going to collect the note?"

"You know."

"Edith told me."

"I am sorry I didn't tell you."

"You should have. I would have discounted Michael's note for you."

I laughed.

"First time you found anything to laugh about."

I was laughing louder. "Funny isn't it? Everyone in this family knew what Michael was. You told me before I married. Not once since I got married, not one of you in ten years has ever said a word against Michael, but you knew his promises were nothing. Edith knew he battered me, but she didn't say anything, not even to Mama. If Mama knew, maybe she would have said, 'Erna, I know what you are going through, we are behind you, we'll help you get your life in order.'"

"You knew how we felt before you got married."

"You could have said something. Anything."

"Between adults marriage is a private contract."

"I am sorry, Dad, I didn't mean to cause you any grief."

"I know, Erna, I know."

"What did Mama say?"

"'Wait till Emmie comes, we'll have a conference.' Time to go in, Erna, too damp out here for an old arthritic."

"You are not old, Papa."

"I am old, Erna. Not as old as Harry Schwartz, but old enough to retire." And Papa laughed.

"What's so funny, Papa?"

"I never thought I would live this long. I never thought I would live to get home, see you, Edith, grow up."

"Papa."

"What?"

"Nothing. Papa, tomorrow, I'll get Emmie."

"Fine. You know what, Erna?"

"What, Papa?"

"It went too fast, too fast to understand, so fast, soon all finished. Poof, just like that."

"What are you talking about, Papa?"

"Life, Erna. Life."

Chapter 11

Erna

The Southwest Regional Airport was three clogged lanes, passengers incoming and departing, unloading and loading, no standing, van pickup for auto rental only. Transportation, limousines, taxis, police. Police double-parked in the second lane, no standing in the third bypass lane, traffic limited to public transportation vehicles.

Dad's Lincoln went into the first of the handicapped spaces, the wheelchair placard on the dashboard. As Dad says, "It's the only advantage of being handicapped I can find so far." Dad refuses to apply for handicapped license plates. "For everyone to see, I'll wait until I am in a wheelchair." This makes Mom most unhappy.

"Robert, don't talk like that."

There is a description of the approach to the Southwest Regional Airport in John Updike's *Rabbit at Rest,* how you drive by a little lake and natural grasses, then the road winds through a nature reserve where Mama's neighbor swears he saw two panther cubs, orange with spots, coming out of the mangroves.

Emmie's flight is announced. In the arrival lounge it is mostly the elderly suntanned in tennis dresses, sweat suits, tan walking shorts, Reeboks, who crowd the "Ticket bearer only beyond this" barrier, waiting for their children, grandchildren.

A full family reunion for a week or two. Emmie is coming through the security gate. Tall, dark hair, blue eyes—we all have blue eyes—five-ten and thinner, taller than any of us, two tennis rackets in her left hand, a duffel bag over her shoulder. In jeans, tennis shoes, whatever brand is this year's best, red cotton crewneck sweater. Emmie doesn't stop, puts her arms around me, kisses my cheek.

"Let's go."

"No luggage?"

"Easy on, easy off with a Nike duffel bag."

"You seem happy."

"Bernie and I won the mixed doubles."

"You tore Bernie away from his microscope?"

"Me and his doctor. Bernie has to take more exercise. Tennis forty minutes, three, four times a week or it's pills for Bernie."

"What's the matter with Dr. Schwartz?"

"Cholesterol, his family curse."

"It's better than diabetes."

"Who has diabetes?"

"It was only my attempt at humor."

We are walking to the car. "Erna, I am hot. I am always surprised how hot Florida is in January."

"You have been coming here for nine years for the weeks between Christmas and January 15."

"I am a slow learner."

"When are you going back, Erna? Maybe we could go together."

"We'll see after the family's annual meeting. You are on the agenda. I haven't told Dad anything about your 'political ambitions.'"

"Somebody has to do it, Erna. I have the time, Papa

and Mama have the money. Papa and Mama support worthy causes. I am a worthy cause. 'Emma Schwartz for Congress, a thinking, caring candidate to represent the Thirty-first Congressional district.'"

"You look too much like a yuppie."

"At least I don't look too Jewish."

"Jewish is in."

"Erna, stop at Walgreens."

"What do you need?"

"Going to buy some Korbel champagne for Edith."

"We need all the support we can get."

Walgreens is on the way to the beach. I am parked, running the air-conditioning.

"Three bottles at twelve dollars a bottle. Dad will kill me. I can hear him: 'If you have to waste your money on Korbel, buy it wholesale.'"

"Dad is right. You paid forty percent too much to Walgreens."

"What's with you and Michael?"

"Settlement is signed, sealed, and delivered."

"Where are you going to live?"

"I got the house."

"Good going, older sister."

"Game for our side. How did you manage that?"

"'Michael, my boy, either I get the house or I call the Feds.'"

"You didn't."

"There is a war out there, Emmie."

"Doing good, Erna baby. Three-fifty for the house. A hundred thousand from Dad. That will get you started. Do Mom and Dad know about the house?"

"About the divorce, yes; about the house, no. Everybody has to live somewhere. The house is not really an asset because when I sell the house, I have to buy a condo in Paris."

The rain, sudden, severe, caught us on Summerlin Road. The window wipers on high could only clear the visibility to fifteen feet.

"Erna, slow down."

"Not to worry. Anti-lock brakes."

"You are crazy to drive this fast. What if one of these geriatrics plows into you?"

"You worry too much, just like Dad, like Mama. Say, when are you going to become a mama? Thirty-six and holding: You have to reach a decision. Emmie, time and tide wait for no man. Sorry, Emmie, no: *woman*."

"All scheduled, dear. If I win the election in 1992, it's baby in 1993, reelection in '94. How could the voters turn out a mother and infant?"

"What if you lose?"

"If I lose, it's baby in '93."

"That's cutting it pretty close."

"Well, if I don't get the nomination, I could manage '92."

I laughed.

"You are in a good mood."

"I just thought of something. Tell the folks you are contemplating motherhood and then ask them for your hundred thousand dollars. They will crumble under the hopes of becoming grandparents."

"You could tell the same story, Erna."

"They wouldn't believe me—motherhood without a husband."

"You could get a donor."

"A lover would be better."

"You are in a good mood."

"Getting better all the time, the closer I get to Paris." I sing *April in Paris*. "Chestnuts in blossom . . ."

"Your voice stinks."

"Now, now. See, at the end of every rain there is

sunshine." The rain had quit as we started onto the causeway. The pelicans dived, fished. The laughing gulls followed each dive to get a remnant, a morsel the pelican had lost. The heat reflected from the roadway; the pelicans rode the thermals over the railing to dive into San Marcos Bay. The Intercoastal bridge across the bay was open. I waited with the motor running.

"Shut the motor, Erna. Save gas. Soon Americans may be dying to protect Kuwaiti oil sheiks."

"Dad says there will be a war."

"Have you ever talked to Dad about Korea? You promised me you would."

"I had other things on my mind."

"I know. A hundred thousand dollars."

There is no sense telling Emmie about Michael's note due in 1996. Dad said Michael's note was of doubtful value. I'll tell Emmie in '96, if and when I collect it. Edith knows, that's enough. "Emmie, from now on I'll have more time and we can see more of each other."

"Best thing you ever did."

"What?"

"Getting rid of Michael."

"Since the divorce no one can say a kind word about Michael."

"All right, Michael is not a bad French cook. He makes a mean *canard l'orange*, but he is pricey."

"He never made you pay."

"Bernie always paid for the drinks. That's where the profits are."

"Not the way you and Bernie drink."

"How is Dad?"

"Mom is worried. She thinks Dad has a progressive nerve loss in his legs and arms. If you ask me, Dad has too much on his mind. But I can't see any nerve loss."

"Dad say anything?"

"Only in Yiddish to Mama."

The sailboat had cleared the opened causeway bridge, headed into the Sonesta Harbor marina. The bridge down, it's on to the island, it's left at the Hilton, then right. There were Mom and Dad and Edith on the porch, waiting, lined up to kiss Emmie. Mama in the lead, then Dad, then Edith. "Welcome, long time no see." Edith hugged Emmie. "Tomorrow, tennis at nine. I reserved a court."

"You recovered enough to take me on?"

"Don't make fun of your oldest sister. Be respectful."

"Mom told me you were having knee trouble."

"A week on pills, a week in the sun, my knee is good enough to beat you."

"Edie, dear, you are getting too old to play singles."

"I'll take an extra Motrin."

"How is Bernie?" From Dad.

"He has to get his cholesterol down."

"The exercise should help." Dad's addition to Emmie's statement.

"Now you are practicing medicine?" This from Mom.

"Millie, if you would read the Tuesday science page in *The New York Times*, you too could keep up with the diseases of the day."

"How are you feeling, Dad?"

"Good, Emmie, really good. That's the short version. Emmie, if you really want to hear—"

Before Dad can finish Mom has answered, "It's nice for us to be outdoors. In Rock City we would be freezing."

Emmie's duffle bag went into the guest closet without unpacking. Emmie was next door at Mom and Dad's, so I followed her.

There she was sitting at the dining room table with Edith, Dad, and Mom, drinking orange juice.

Emmie is a direct hitter. As soon as I come in, sit down, she is making her points. "Now that we are all together . . .

Togetherness is what it is all about. I can run for Congress—that is, I think I can get the nomination. I have the support of the party chairman. My program is acceptable. It fits in with the needs of our district. I am a personable candidate, with the proper qualifications, background education. I have served my time on the volunteer boards, now if I can get your support."

Dad laughed. "With my hands I can't stuff envelopes."

This was my opportunity. "Emmie needs our economic support, money she can draw on after her committee 'TO ELECT SCHWARTZ' has used up all the PAC funds."

"Where did you learn from politics, Erna?"

"Business is in politics. Our company pays and then we wait. I did legislative coordination for the mortgage association. We wait until there is a bill our industry is interested in and then I call on the congressman that took our donation. 'Mr. Congressman, because of the slowdown in housing construction, our industry believes that retaining the fourteen percent annual depreciation schedule for rehabbed property is now more important than ever.'"

Edith applauded. "You two doing a sister act? The Kramer Girls before the funding committee."

"If Emmie gets the nomination, I'm going to help."

Emmie laughed. "Erna is going to be my bagwoman."

"You know what you are getting into so, tell how much?"

"I have it all here, Dad. National will help. I think one hundred thousand dollars would do. I think it would be money well spent."

"It would be better than losing it on a bankrupt bank in New England." That support from Mom.

"If Emmie wins we have an advocate and if she loses she has the experience of trying" was my add-on.

"We will have to get certain guarantees, Emmie." Dad is chuckling; that's a positive.

"It's a risk, Dad, what guarantees?"

"If you get elected, you won't raise taxes for the rich."

"Income tax is progressive, Dad, you know that. Redistribution is what it's about."

"Emmie it's the investment of capital that makes for jobs. High taxes, less to invest."

Edith also laughed. "O.K., you have my support. Join a growth industry, go to Washington, make more jobs for the underprivileged."

"It's my damn Jewish guilt. O.K., I vote yes, put in your social programs. I vote to take from the rich, give to the underprivileged. Give it to the Afro-Americans, or is it the blacks this year: Give your deprived more than equal opportunity."

Mom interrupted Edith. "Salmon tonight O.K.?" That stopped Edith's *You can't legislate equality, you have to earn it, gain it through education, through improving motivation. We tried at the bank.* Edith and Dad: Edith is on her way to becoming a Dad replica? Equal opportunity is fine, but no more than equal.

More than equal takes from someone else's equality. "What you gain by preferences diminishes your accomplishments, makes your colleagues scoff. Make opportunities to work to be self-sufficient and then you have a taxpayer. Look, what this country needs is more taxpayers."

Mom's intervention had saved our roundtable from another political quarrel. Emmie verses Edith.

"Tonight we drink Korbel."

"You came prepared for a victory celebration."

"Only twelve dollars a bottle at Walgreens."

"Don't let Dad hear you. Tell him you brought the champagne from California."

"You want to help Mama?"

"Tonight's dinner is my treat. From tomorrow on it's all yours."

Dad was still smiling. Dad kissed Emmie on the head.

"Congratulations, Congesswoman."

"Not yet."

"Winning is all in the preparation, Emmie. Define your goals, organize, execute." Dad left for the porch, and his writing. I put my arm around Emmie, whispered, "You didn't have to promise a grandchild. You can use that gambit if you need an extra hundred thousand."

"Always one step ahead, aren't you, Erna?

"Like Dad, define your goals, organize, execute."

"Quit making fun of dear Dad."

"I know he means well. He loves us."

"Why does he have to direct us. Does he think we are stupid?"

Edith had heard that. "Dad is giving us instructions to protect us from the cruel world. He is the male model of his generation."

"My God, you have gained perfect insight."

"Thanks, Erna." Edith kissed my head just like Dad. She was chuckling. For Edith to laugh, that's great progress.

Chapter 12

Erna

On the telephone, Emmie is telling Bernie, "Like I said, Bernie, it was really easier than I thought it would be. I didn't have to present my platform. So far, so good. I really thought that Edith would complain. I could hear Edith shoot me down: "Throwing good money down the social service drain. We would be better off just giving the money to the Salvation Army for all the good a freshman congresswoman from California can do in Washington."

Emmie is the sister that confidence built. By the time she was born things were easier at the Kramers. Mama had help at the office. Papa was home from the Army. You get Mama aside, talking about getting started, "the old days," she'll tell you about Papa and me and Edith. "Your dad was away. He didn't know he had a daughter named Erna until you were four. The first year Papa came home. It wasn't easy for your father. He really wasn't all that well."

"In what way, Mama?"

"One day I'll tell you. It turned out all right, that's all that counts."

Emmie never had to ask Mama, "When is Papa coming home?"

Emmie missed the visits to the VA hospital in Iowa City. Papa walking around Iowa City, his arm around Mama, me in a stroller and Edith pushing me. "Erna, you listen to Edith. You stay in the stroller." It was down by the river where the Art Museum is now that Papa first held me, threw me up to the sky. "So, you are Erna. Prettier than your picture. Been a good girl, not giving your mama any troubles? Your mama has been through enough." That was my introduction to Papa's instructions, a warning, so I went to Edith.

"What has Mama been through?"

"I don't know, Erna. Go watch TV"

"Edith, tell me."

"You are too little."

So, I began to cry. I guess I was asking too many questions or crying too much, because I ended up at the all-day nursery school. Or maybe it was because Emmie was coming and with Edith in school Mama could devote more time to Emmie. Sometimes I am sure it's because we had no father when we were growing up that not one of the Kramer girls has children. Then I am sure it's because if we had children our husbands would leave and we would be forced to raise them all alone. Then I think: Why blame Dad?

Blame our careers. Kids get in the way of our careers. We were all going to be so successful, more successful than Mom and Dad. Edith was to be president of a bank by the time she was forty, and me, I was going to have it all, a house in San Francisco, a condo in Tahoe, August in France. For Emmie, it's simple; she wants to perform deeds of loving kindness, feed the hungry, house the poor and underprivileged. Emmie had a red Opel convertible when she was at Northwestern. When she graduated, she gave the car back to Dad. "That's not the kind of car I need to go to work in the southside of Chicago."

Emmie is the confident one. Listen to her and Bernie's plans: Congresswoman in '92, a child in '93. So sure they will have a child.

Erna, you could have had a child, with Michael.

No, thank you.

So, why did you stay for ten years?

Hope. I had hopes it would get better. Sometimes it was almost good — that's what raises your hopes — that and not wanting to tell Mama, "You were right all along, Mama. I have known for years you were right about Michael, but people do change." Michael didn't.

For that matter, I don't think Frank really treats Edith all that well, either. It's just that Edith fights back. Twenty years of taming Frank and he still flares up at Dad. "That was a stupid risk." Poor Mama, she really hadn't been lucky with her sons-in-law; neither has Dad, really. Oh, Frank will play an occasional round of golf with him. Papa doesn't have a son-in-law to reminisce with. "When I was a boy in Poland . . ." or "I worked my way through college as a Fuller Brush man."

I have heard Frank laugh at Papa, behind his back, of course, laugh, scoff. "Edith, when your dad made his money everybody was making twice as much." He laughs and takes Dad's money.

I am sure it's not like Dad pictured his three daughters married to Jewish boys with intellectual parents whom he would invite to Seders in Rock City. Nor did he get blue-eyed, red-haired grandchildren, or even his own daughters coming home for advice. "Papa, should we?" "Should I . . .?" "Papa, which graduate school should I go to?" "Papa, which job shall I take?"

Not a one of us ever discussed anything with Dad but dollars — at least I never did. "Dad, I need a hundred thousand dollars to start a gallery in Paris."

"Sure, Erna, why not?"

"Dad, I want to run for Congress. A hundred thousand will do for now."

"Sure, Emma, why not."

Good old Dad. One thing he didn't do is use money as a weapon. "Marry Michael and not a penny." I'm not so sure he shouldn't have. Reward and punishment modifies behavior in mice and children. It may have improved mine, but I doubt it, because I was out to do it on my own like Mama and Papa had done. . . .It's not too late, Erna. Go tell your father, your mother, "Mama, Papa, I know it wasn't easy, you did the best you could. Look at us, Mama, we didn't turn out so badly."

Emma has finally hung up the phone. "Emmie, how is Bernie getting along without . . ."

"Say it, Erna. *Without my direction.*" For your information, Erna, Bernie has learned to use the microwave."

"He better be careful. I hear the waves make men sterile. Something about killing their sperm."

"Just so it doesn't kill his desire."

"You never told me he was that good in bed."

"You know me, Erna. I don't like to brag in front of my sisters."

Mama called on the telephone, "Supper."

Mama was tired or she would have walked over.

"How does Mama look to you, Emmie?"

"I don't think she is sleeping well. She say what's bothering her?"

"You know Mama, from Mama all you get is, 'It's great to have you all here. It's good to be a family again. What do you want for lunch?'"

"I'm going to get Mama to go for a walk with me. I'll bet she'll tell me."

"Good luck, Emmie. You find out, tell me. I have given up."

Emmie. Emmie is like Papa and Mama, organized. Jogging before breakfast, then only healthful, high-bulk cereal, Grape-nuts, skim milk for breakfast. That she learned from Papa. Emma has enthusiasm and faith, otherwise how could she keep talking about tax benefits to supplement the earnings of the working poor. Not for Emma to question how are you going to get the poor to work when they are better off on the handouts. Emma is a believer — increase opportunities for education and employment, provide child care, attract business to the inner city, then poverty and disorder will disappear. Papa and Mama have never said a discouraging word to Emmie.

Papa just gives her his cut-outs, each *New York Times* headline proclaiming another social effort failure. The rich are not supporting institutions that serve the poor. Emmie reads Papa's missives and smiles. "Look at you, Papa. You lost your lawsuit; you never got to build in Prarie Junction. That was prejudice against your open housing. You did build housing for the elderly."

The folks are overwhelmed by the thought of Emmie being elected to Congress. "Our daughter, the Congresswoman." I can just see it, "The Kramer Foundation for the Education of the Deprived." A couple of hundred thousand dollars of our inheritance to bring cultural enrichment to Emmie's downtrodden, underprivileged suppporters. All to be administered by Emma Kramer Schwartz, your Congresswoman. Saturday afternoon art classes; on Sunday afternoon, Afro-American music concerts. Health clubs with cultural overtones: "Learn to tap dance, or stepdance with the Robinson Brothers." Trips to art museums in the white minivan with the lettering proclaiming, "A Kramer Foundation Project."

Mama wouldn't permit the signage, but she might go for the "enrichment," maybe not during Emmie's first term, but if she was to be re-elected. "Erna, our money is going to make taxpayers," is what Papa would say. Edith is the key, the swing vote. Mama and Papa and Edith make three, so if Edith says no, all will be inherited and none will be wasted, except for the usual small gifts each year, a couple of hundred to Papa's college, Mama's charities. Edith is the key to our inheritances, inheritance enhancement through the magic of compounding. Erna, quit projecting threatening scenarios. "Yes, Doctor . . .You are quite right, Doctor, but, Doctor, Mom and Dad could give all their money away to good causes, and I would be left on my own . . ." "Mrs. Vevers, there is nothing in your parents' previous behavior for you to create these fears."

That is why I didn't leave Michael. I was afraid of being on my own. It took me six years to conquer that. Now how long will it take to overcome the fear being disinherited, a child, a daughter discarded.

"It's all up to you, Mrs. Vevers."

"Erna, you want to play tennis?"

"Emmie, you play with Edith. I'm going for a walk with Dad."

We came home to be a family. I knew how Mama's little mind worked, so that when Papa and I are gone you girls will have each other. At least once a year you'll come together. Ten days in the Florida sun to bring the Kramer girls together forever, forever, until death do us part. Not like in Papa's family where Papa got nothing and his sisters got all. Really, there was so little there is nothing to talk about, but I have heard Mama: "All Papa wanted was just a memento from his mother or his father. He has nothing. Sure, he has the letters he received when he was in the Army." The Kramer inheritance will be handled equitably. All will share equally, all as stipulated in a will drawn by the finest estate planning attorneys in Chicago. "You know all that, Mrs. Vevers. Why are you so concerned about your inheritance? Mrs. Vevers, you could always talk to your dad."

"Dad, time for your walk on the beach. It's that time of the year again." Dad is surprised, looks up from his writing.

"Yesterday Edith took me out for a stroll. Today it's you."

"Once a year isn't too often."

"You missed last year, Erna."

"O.K., I owe you one."

"Erna, I want to show you something." We walked east on the road behind the cottages. Dad turned left at the second lane that goes over the canal. "There on the top of the Norwegian pine, an osprey nest."

I said, "How interesting."

"We could go to the bird sanctuary one evening, Erna. Mom and I saw the Roseate spoonbills feeding in the backwater ponds. That's a first for us. Usually they are out in the tidal flats, so far out we can't watch them without binoculars. Yesterday, Mom and I got within thirty feet of them."

"Dad, how are you feeling?"

"Good enough."

"Dad, why so busy, working, writing?"

"Running out of time, Erna. Edith explained it all to me. She did a study. It takes sixteen years to become a successful writer. I have been writing for six years. In ten more years I am world famous. I have published six great novels, several wonderful plays. I am eligible for the Pulitzer Prize, the National Book Award, even the Nobel. *The New York Times* calls me, 'Robert Kramer, you have been nominated for the Nobel.' I don't want it to be too late."

"Too late for what?"

"Too late for me to answer the reporters' questions intelligently."

"Dad, you are not losing your head. Your head is perfectly good."

"So far so good."

"Mom is worried about you."

"I know. She thinks I could do better about dropping things. I have told her I am doing the best I can. 'No, you are not, Robert, you can do better,' is what I get from your mother. I try, Erna, but I don't think I can."

"You are walking well."

"It's one of my good days."

"Dad, I am sorry if I caused you any grief, about my divorce."

"Nothing to apologize for, Erna."

We walked back on the low tide beach. Dad returned to his writing, and I helped Mama prepare lunch, just the usual, yogurt and salad, and cheese and sardines, bagels and coffee. Mama makes the prettiest salads. The onions on the right of the centered lettuce leaves color balanced by the quartered tomatoes on the left. The tan mushrooms are opposite the sliced forest green and red peppers. Edith has that knack, too.

"Mama, I went for a walk with Dad."

"He likes that. Dad is very proud of his daughters. I am, too, of course." Mama put her arms around me.

"So, why don't you tell us?"

"Tell you what?"

"Tell me how you feel about me, if there is anything I can do to help."

"You have your own life, Erna."

"Edith gets to help."

"It's only because she lives closer. I'll tell you something, Erna. Dad doesn't like to burden Edith with his problems, either."

"So, why did you make her the executor?"

"Not that again, Erna. Edith is the oldest. It's not that we don't trust you or your business judgment. It's that we see Edith every couple of months. That's all there is to it."

"I know, Mama. You and Papa meant well, but why don't you ever ask us, let us reach the decisions that will affect us."

"Bring it up at the next 'board meeting,' Erna. I think your father and I would be delighted with your willingness to take up increased responsibilities. You had better explain how you are going to manage that from Paris."

When it came to "family business," Mama was no better than Papa, slow to innovate, very slow to share the decision-making process, unwilling to build depth of management, just not willing to acknowledge it's time for them both to quit, time for the Kramer Girls to take over. Edith will never say that, and Emmie is too much into herself. Still, I could try to get Edith to introduce "increased responsibilities for daughters in the Kramer Companies." Papa will listen to Edith before he begins his sermons, begins talking about himself. That's all he does, talk about himself.

"Mama, do you want me to go shopping with you?"

"I promised to go with Emmie to the library. Your turn tomorrow. Anything special you want for lunch? We are going to the fish store. Grouper O.K.?"

That's what Mama did talk about, food—breakfast, lunch, dinner—anything but what I want.

Chapter 13

Erna

Dad never goes out in the noonday sun. Edith will sit covered up on the beach in her black one-piece bathing suit reading or writing. If one of the neighbor kids turns up the radio she comes in, muttering, "Damn noise." Dad doesn't hear her, but I do. "Edith, you are beginning to sound like Mama."

"Sorry, Erna, can't stand the noise. I am going swimming. You have any laundry you want done?" (The laundry room is in the pool house.)

"I'll get it. I'll go with you."

"Dad, if I get a call, I'll call back." Edith brings Dad the cordless telephone from his bedroom.

"Put the phone back, Edith. I'll answer the one in the kitchen. It's good for me to get up. Doctor says I have to get up every hour on the hour."

The swimming pool was Mama's joy, delight, heated to eighty-five or eighty-six degrees. Mama, her head encased in a white cap, goes up and back in her modified back stroke with frog kick, and arms to the side. Then Mama does her aquatic exercises, leg lifts, knee lifts, left arm over head, right arm over head. There is a large clock on the pool wall. Mama swam exactly forty minutes except for the days she did her laundry. Then she swam exactly thirty minutes, the time it took for the wash to spin dry. Mama never swam the forty-five minutes the dryer requires to complete its cycle; that would have invaded her schedule.

Edith must prepare to swim: Cap, goggles, checks her waterproof watch, begins her freestyle laps. For me, a few up and back breast strokes, a few crawls, a few underwater passes are sufficient. The sun through the screening reflects from the pool floor; the rays break up into swirls, and concentric circles. I surface, dive, glide through to destroy the ripples that reform by the time I kick off the pool wall to again destroy the perfect circles.

I wait for Edith. She has tossed the laundry into the dryer. At poolside there are two white plastic lounge chairs and a matching white, round plastic table with four plastic armchairs. Edith is gathering her cover-up from the tables. Her torso is wrapped in a bath towel. From the back she is beginning to look like Mama.

Why not? Mama was only twenty-one when Edith was born.

"Mrs. Vevers, talk to your dad if you are worried about your inheritance. I can understand your father's reluctance to quit. Your dad does not seem manipulative. You have to understand that business is his life."

"Edith, take the cover-up off, sit down here, feel the sun."

"Sun causes cancer. You know that Mama has had two skin cancers removed from her thigh."

"Trust your sunscreen, believe in Walgreens."

Edith laughs. "If I can't believe in Walgreens, what can I believe in. Thanks for the Korbel. You should try the Domaine Chandon Brut, cheaper and better."

"You quoting Michael."

"No, *The New York Times*."

"You and Dad."

Edith has taken off her cover-up, eases herself into the armchair across the table from me, begins to rub her knee.

"No better?"

"No worse. I guess the pills helped. Papa and I are taking the same pills."

"It's only old age, Edith."

"You'll find out, Erna. The knees are the first to go."

"Not if I don't play tennis."

"You ought to exercise more."

"Next time around I'll marry a health freak instead of a chef."

"Anybody in mind?"

"Nothing but rejects out there, rejects and health freaks in love with their own body. I'm learning, Edith."

"You still going to the marriage counselor?"

"I don't even know why we tried counseling. What surprised me was that Michael was willing to go. It must have been a convenient time for him."

"Don't be so damn cynical, Erna. Maybe he wanted to save your marriage."

"All he had to do was keep his hands off me."

"Abusing you?"

"Using me."

"Erna, I don't want to go into that. You have your problems, I have mine."

"With Frank. I never thought you two would stay, you with that Okie."

"Your prejudices are showing, Erna."

"Sorry, Edith."

"That's O.K. I don't like Michael. I guess when it comes to husbands neither one of us is a big winner."

"You sound like Papa, Edith: Average earnings is all you get. Many times we are lucky to get that."

"Average wasn't going to be good enough for us, remember, Edith?"

"I guess Emmie did the best with Bernie. That's because he doesn't fight her."

"A good fight now and then isn't all that bad. I don't mind that. I'm sure as hell not going to stand for Frank putting a hand on me. The first time he does that, out he goes. I told him that twenty years ago."

"Frank isn't going to lose the future value of the Kramer Companies by hitting you. He isn't that stupid. I tried warning Michael, didn't do me a bit of good."

"You should have thrown him out or left."

"Now you tell me. Why didn't you tell me years ago?"

"You got yours, Erna. I have mine."

Edith is checking her watch. The pool clock tells me two minutes and ten seconds before the sheets would be dry.

"I'm going to take out the sheets. I'm not running off, Erna. I'll be right back. I know you have something you want to talk about."

Edith moved her chair into the shade. We were face to face close. "Edith, I need your counsel."

"That's new."

"Let me talk. Don't interrupt, don't do a Papa on me."

"O.K., talk."

"Don't you think we should be more involved in reaching decisions about the Kramer Companies. After all, it is our money."

"O.K. with me, but it's not that simple. The folks have divided their estate into three parts. The trust officers run the liquid assets. Dad and Mom run the art collection. That is, Dad runs it and Mom knows what's going on. Mom does the daily cash management. Dad hasn't written a check in five years, unless you call paying his typists writing checks. That leaves the real estate. I don't know how you and I can help manage real estate in Rock City when you are in California or Paris and I'm in Chicago."

"That's why I think Mama should sell the cottages. Then the condo could be in our names. Dad and Mom could rent from us.

"That could have a gift tax problem. The condo is Mama's; she gives us a condo share, that's a gift. You can't have it all, Erna. If you take the annual cash, you can't have a condo share. Anyway, Mama may not want to sell the cottages. You know Mama—she is sure it's the cottages that are going to keep us together. I wouldn't be surprised to find Mama has set aside an incentive, a bonus for early arrival for the annual Kramers-in-Florida reunion. It makes Mama happy."

"Edith."

"What?"

"What if I don't make it in Paris? I am afraid. I have never been on my own."

"It's that time, Erna. No reason you shouldn't succeed. All right, so you fail, so what? Papa is out a hundred thousand."

"It's not the money, Edith. It's another couple of years out of my life."

"What would you rather be doing? If this is what you want, go for it."

"I'm afraid of failing."

"Who isn't?"

"I don't want to fail."

"Quit worrying. You are a Kramer in the great tradition of Ma and Pa Kramer who ran their lives with no idea of the risks they were taking. Papa got better than average earnings. Don't let his slogan fool you. In twenty years Papa has had four gains, two losses, and those losses . . .Well, against the percentage of gain were losses from winnings. Trouble was the losses, one after the other, hurt Papa's pride, Papa's faith in himself in his 'wisdom.' That's our trouble, Erna, risk analysis. We understand the risk—

too much education, so we worry. Papa just knew it had to be done. Once he started, he had to complete. Too many choices for us, Erna."

"You sound like my counselor."

Edith laughed. "So you lose a hundred thousand. That's my thirty-three thousand dollar gift to you. Emmie will never notice. She has Bernie Schwartz's money."

"What if I fail?"

"Well, your French will be better, you can take early retirement, write a book about your experiences. You can join the writing Kramers, like the Brontes. Papa and Mama will support you."

"I want to make it on my own."

"Who doesn't?" Edith put her arm around me. "Erna, there ain't no hundred percent of nothing. That's what they say in Oklahoma."

"What about it, shall I volunteer to help Dad manage?"

"You can if you like, but think it over. He takes you up, you are back in Rock City, 'where the Mississippi flows from east to west.' What are you going to do there, read to the old folks at the Jewish Center? If you want to meet an interesting man, you'll have to call me to arrange it for you?"

Edith was folding the sheets, pillow cases, color-coded, tan for the guest cottage, white for Mom and Dad. Edith pushed the wire laundry cart. "Come on, I want to get into the shower."

"It would be better if we were running things, at least it would help the folks."

"I have enough to do. Once a month I get Dad's memos, FYI. Dad hasn't resolved a thing in ten years. Everything is hanging, two IRS reviews, one goes back five years. Two, maybe three lawsuits. Two notes, one due next year, one in 1999."

"I didn't know. Why didn't you tell me?"

"So I told you, what could you do about it? Not go to Paris, give up San Francisco?"

I didn't answer Edith.

Not this year.

"Bring it up, Erna. I think Papa would like that. Show him you care."

"Thanks, Edith."

"For what?"

"For sharing. I hope you didn't think I was complaining."

"No. It may not be a bad idea to speak to Dad. The both of us. There is no harm in talking about . . . about what we'll have to face sooner or later."

"When?"

"As soon as I get out of this wet suit."

"Mama and Emmie aren't back yet. "Do you think it would be best to wait for them?"

"Maybe yes, maybe no. I don't know, Erna. You know Mama, she'll protect Papa. She wants Papa to do less. I'm not as clever as I should be. I hate this family togetherness when we talk about tomorrow. Tomorrow is when Dad and Mom are gone. I'm not ready for that yet."

"Whatever you say, Edith."

"Put it on the agenda under 'for the common good.' It won't go away, Erna, just gets closer. Like Dad says, it's closing in on us."

"What?"

"Life, death. There is the enemy, death, and taxes."

"You sound like an insurance salesman."

"Sooner or later. O.K., Erna, as soon as Mama and Emma get back."

Mama was unpacking the groceries, Emmie putting the skim milk salt-free cottage cheese, the low-fat Gouda cheese in the refrigerator.

"Can I help?"

"There are some gladioli in the car."

"I'll get them."

When I returned Edith was in the dining room, in her cover-up over her second best swimsuit. The same one-piece model as the black, only this one was grey with "thinning" vertical black stripes. Edith looked at the glads.

"You buy those, Emmie?"

"Yes. How did you know?"

"Mama doesn't buy white."

"Why?"

"She knows."

"Knows what?"

"Knows I don't like them. Reminds me of funerals."

"You want me to throw them out?"

"No, just don't buy white, not when I am around."

Mama didn't say anything. Mama had heard.

"White was all there was at Jerry's. I thought white was better than no flowers at all. Dad likes flowers for Shabbus."

"Today is only Thursday, Mama."

"I wasn't planning on going to the store tomorrow."

"Let's forget about the glads, Edith. Mama bought grouper for supper. How about you and I baking some cornbread for Dad. I bought a mix, a low-salt mix."

"Sure."

"Edith."

"O.K., Erna. Emmie, get some orange juice. Time to prepare for our annual meeting."

"You presiding?"

"Equal opportunity, Edith, a round table, from right to left or left to right with a rotating chairman, like at San Francisco State."

"This is a much smaller department, Emmie, I don't

know if your father is willing to give up his chairmanship. You ask him."
"You ask him, Edith. You are the oldest."
"I'm satisfied the way things are."
"Coward."
"Wise, young one."
"No pain, no gain."
"O.K., Emmie, you tell Papa."
"I will."

Chapter 14

Erna

Poor Dad, still being brought up by Mama. "Robert, you can do better." This after Dad had dropped the glass knob of the coffee percolator's cover. "I didn't drop it on purpose, Millie; it just dropped out of my hand."

Edith sees Dad's failure; she is beside me. "Erna, Papa is having troubles grasping."

"Everybody drops things, don't make so much of it."

"This is the third time this week that Papa has . . ."

So, between Mama—who is watching Papa—and Edith—who is watching me watching Dad—it is several days before I can sit down to the left of Dad at his work table. Mom is doing the pool house laundry, Edith is off to the Hilton to send a fax for Dad. After three days of observation I do believe that Dad looks about the same as last year; the only change is that he has been taking a "lie me down" at about three, four o'clock.

"Am I keeping you from your nap?"

"No nap today, Erna. I used espresso as an antidote. Doesn't always work, but today I hope it does."

"What are you so busy with?"

"Getting ready for Leroy Carlson, running comparison studies. Leroy Carlson vs. North American Insurance second-to-die policy. So, that way Edith will have the money to pay the taxes."

"I didn't know you needed so much."

"It's not so much, Erna. It's that we—Edith—will need liquid assets."

Dad had said we and changed to Edith. My oldest sister will be the executor, trustee, administor. Edith will be more than fair. Getting my distributions will take forever, and advances I can forget about unless Edith herself will have a need or Emmie will request a "special distribution." Then it's two against one.

"How are you feeling, Dad?"

Dad laughs. "How can an old man feel?"

"Not so old."

"Old enough to be reverting into infantile sleeping habits, up half the night and then napping in the afternoon like a four-year-old."

"Enjoy it. Harry Schwartz naps every day."

"How do you know?"

"I spent a weekend in Palo Alto with Emmie, and Bernie's dad was there."

"How is Emmie doing?"

"Too many damn causes."

Papa's prayer book is on the glasstop table, the pages torn loose by years of thumbing have been repaired with scotch tape. The Friday night prayers are between sheets of laminate. "Your mother repaired it. I need a new prayer book. Pages forty-nine to fifty-one are missing."

"So why don't you buy yourself one?"

"Can't find one that size at the Jewish Center. Funny, I never get around to doing these little things for myself. Too busy with the big picture of the hereafter."

Dad is up into the kitchen, comes back with a glass of water into which he has squeezed the juice of a yet-to-ripen lime.

"Have to get up every hour or I'm so damn arthritic. Does the nap help Harry Schwartz?"

"He swears by his nap, luxuriates in it, enjoys it."

"Harry is an old man."

"Harry is only three years older than you."

"Harry looks backward. Did he tell you about the trip he took to Israel twenty years ago?"

"Harry has fond memories."

"He is lucky. For me, I can't recall that things were so great. For Mom and me things are better now. We have more choices, more free time, more time for you."

"Choices are difficult for me."

"Run a pro forma A B C and choose."

"About my life?"

"I never did it for my life."

"You always knew what you wanted."

"Immigrants." Dad laughs again. "Jewish immigrants didn't have many choices: Self-employment or government. I tried government, made it work for two and half years, gave it up."

"Why, Dad?"

"No price for failure. You get no success. You just keep going until you take early retirement."

"That's pretty harsh. Prejudicial, I would say."

"Our experiences were different. Do you want to go for a little walk?" Dad loves to walk. To walk he has to stop "working." Harry Schwartz calls Dad a compulsive worker. Dad is not compulsive, just organized; letters get answered in three days. "To be filed" is passed to Mama the day received. His entries are in his journal by the third day. The journal is by his bed in the lower drawer of the night table, waiting for an insightful business concept. "Walk for forty minutes, twenty minutes to the mile-and-a-half marker and back. I'll be right back." Dad returns with his darkest sun glasses—frames from 1950, temples from

1990. Dad throws nothing away. His abraded golf shirts he leaves at the cottage. His "Y" all cotton T-shirt he wears to the pool. His worn-out Reeboks walkers he saves to walk on the wet low-tide mud flats.

We walk east towards the lighthouse, towards a sign, "Open House," on a beachfront cottage on stilts. "Two bedrooms, two bath. Lot 50 x 150. $750,000." Ours is 150 x 150, and Carlson is talking six hundred, seven hundred thousand on a trade. Mama's cottages have a swimming pool.

We walked past the open house to the three-story condominiums. "Our cottages are older."

"What is the difference, Erna, how old they are when they are going to get torn down?" Dad hasn't laughed when he said that. We turn back, and it's Dad who is questioning me. "How did you find Carlson?"

"He came by last January. You and Mom were driving Edith and Emmie to the airport. He left his card. You know, if you ever want to sell."

"Your Mama's cottages. You called him?"

"Carlson offered me a three percent finder's fee."

"You didn't tell me."

"We haven't sold yet. Dad, I need some money, money all my own."

"In my count you have received one hundred and sixty thousand in the last eight years."

"I put it into the restaurant."

"Take it out."

"Michael has it invested in Banyuls. He bought a hotel—dollars against francs. It doesn't buy that much in France."

"How much do you need?"

"A couple of hundred thousand."

We returned to the beach in front of the cottages where Dad keeps a plastic armchair, a chair that he can get out of without help. Dad sits down. I am at his feet on the sand. The gulls are laughing. The sandpipers are diligently splitting coquinas at the shoreline, retreating as the surf comes in, returning to the shell splitting when the surf leaves. Dad watches the terns rise, circle, return to the beach. "Have you told your mother?"

"No."

"All right, tell me." I am the little girl at Dad's feet, waiting to tell him , *Edith made me. Mama said I had to. I don't want to, Daddy. Tell them I don't have to.* "It's Michael. He has been putting everything into the hotel. It sounded like a good idea. The Germans are building on the coast just ten, fifteen miles north of Banyuls, a perfect place to invest in to offset the dollar, fixing up a little each year. That's what Michael has been doing."

"I thought you said we."

"You know how Michael is, old-country ways. Everything is in his name in Banyuls. He is the French citizen. That's how he explained it would be easier to do business."

"It was your money, Erna."

"I don't want to go into it. I don't want to hear I told you so. I am getting a divorce. I'll get a hundred thousand from Michael as a settlement. I get a hundred thousand from sale of the cottages." That and eighteen thousand from Leroy Carlson. "That will do me until I can get the art gallery started in Paris. I have some wonderful artists willing to go with me, Dad. Nathan Olivera said he would go with me, and so did Lester Johnson. I have a complete business plan."

"Erna, Erna."

"It's not a tragedy, Dad."

Dad has his hand on my head.

"I tried, I tried. I loved Michael when I married him. Anyway, I thought I did until . . . Well, you see Michael at his best. Michael has an awful temper. All right, I wasted ten years. I am forty years old, Daddy, forty."

Dad got up, gave me his hand to help me to his feet. "It's not easy, Erna, being alone."

"Everyone is alone, Dad. Everyone."

"You can always try family. Don't get agitated over money; it's not worth it."

"Not if you don't have it."

"O.K., Erna. I'll talk to Mama. Then you talk to Edith. Edith has good sense. One evening when Emmie is here we'll sit down and hear you for American contemporary art."

"Dad, I could sell off the Picabia interwoven figures painting for you. You would save the twenty percent you pay Sothebys."

"Not so fast, *mein kind*, my child." When Dad is upset he reverts to Yiddish, his first language, the language he spoke until he was seven or eight, when he came to Rock City. Mama saw us come down to the beach. She and Dad went for their evening walk east and then west into the sunset. Dad wouldn't tell her this evening, "Erna is getting a divorce." No, he wouldn't tell her until they were in bed, together, so that Mama could cry before she fell asleep. Do mothers still cry when their forty-year-old daughter gets a divorce?

I sat down in Dad's chair, listened to the gulls laugh, to the constancy of the surf. Forty. Forty wasn't all that great.

The contemporary art market was shot in the USA. Last fall's New York auction sales prices were down. For the American artists I was going to introduce in Paris, it didn't matter all that much because they had never been that up. Lester Johnson was in his late sixties, and Olivera was only a little younger. They have solid reputations; with Dad's Johnson collection, twenty, twenty-five paintings, drawings, watercolors, if Johnson caught on in Paris I could sell a couple of Dad's pieces a year. I would make the folks rich, not as rich as the Sculls, or the Schlumbergers, who got millions for Jasper Johns and Raushcenbergs. Dad hadn't said yes, but he hadn't said no. Emmie was with me. "I could use the money, Erna." Let Emmie tell them why. Edith would be difficult. Mom? Impossible to assess. For the sale of the cottages: Erna, yes; Emma, yes; Edith, present; Dad, unknown. Mama, I would have to vote a no. I can hear my father telling Mama, "Best thing that ever happened to Erna."

Mama never liked Michael. A *gruber goy* she had called him. "What's a *gruber goy*, Dad?"

"A country boy, a sort of 'rough around the edges' fellow."

It was my Uncle Will who told me, "A boor, an oaf." A gentile without culture or manners. My Uncle Will had been suspicious.

"You studying Yiddish, Erna?"

"I have been reading Rosten. He didn't quite explain it."

The crow cawed, *Gruber goy, gruber goy.* Mama was more than right. "It's a different value system, Erna. I am not talking about religion, Erna."

"Mama, you were right. I should have listened to you."

"Erna, you never listened to me; don't start now."

"Mama, I should have walked out sooner, when I found out that Michael was skimming the cash from the restaurant, taking the money back to France with him every August when he closed down, investing in that old hotel by the railroad station. It was a bargain purchase, but the rehab was expensive and the location was lousy. Tourists now come by cars down the coastal highway, not by the railroad. There are new hotels all along the corniche. 'It's not the Ritz, Erna, but a great place to hide our money.' I don't know why I didn't leave then."

Edith was next. Dad's warning: *Once you have a plan, act. Don't delay. It doesn't get easier.* Edith always knew before I told her. How she knew, I don't know. The sooner I tell Edith the better.

Edith was reading *The New York Times*, sitting at Papa's desk in Papa's armchair, her elbows on the table like Dad, jotting numbers on a legal pad. I sat beside her. That's where I started an hour ago, me in the chair beside Dad's "work table."

Now it's me and Edith, then Mama. "I told Dad."

"What?"

"I told Dad I would like to start a gallery in Paris, strictly American contemporary—Olivera, Lester Johnson, maybe Marcia Relli. If I'm lucky, Philip Guston. I need a hundred thousand as an advance from our inheritance."

"Don't go talking as if the folks are going to die tomorrow. You know I can't handle that."

"It's only a hundred thousand, and Michael is going to give me a hundred thousand."

"From his skimmings." Edith has a real ugly streak at times, more than cynicism.

"How do you know Michael skims?"

"I know restaurants, Erna. In goes your good money, out goes the cash to France. Dear Michael going to be your partner, going to invest with you?"

"No, I am on my own. You might just as well know I'm getting a hundred thousand as a divorce settlement."

"You lost sixty thousand and ten years, Erna. I always thought you were smarter than that."

"I didn't want to fight."

"He beat it out of you?"

I began to cry. How did Edith know? How did Edith always know? "How did you find out?"

"Emmie told me."

"She promised."

"You know Emmie. She was doing a good deed by telling me. I was supposed to save you."

"Why didn't you?"

"You are a big girl, Erna. You makes your bed, you sleeps in it." Edith put her arms around me. "All you had to do was tell me. I would have done what I could. Why didn't you?"

"Would you believe it, I was ashamed."

"Ashamed of what, failing again, with that pig?"

"You never did like Michael."

"What's to like? I can't stand him, not since I heard way he spoke to old Mr. Krouse."

"You sound like Dad and Mama."

"That's not all bad, Erna."

"Edith, about the hundred thousand just for me."

"We'll see."

"I have to know."

"Emmie will be here. Carlson is coming on Thursday. I think you'll know before you go back."

"Edith, how did you know about Michael skimming?"

"I was a loan officer for ten years. Restaurants were my specialty. How much has dear Michael been laundering in Banyuls, in his own name of course?"

"About a hundred and fifty thousand a year."

"Pretty soon that's money. Six or eight years, more than a million all stuck into a hotel."

"So he says."

"Marry a cheat, you get cheated. You can get ten percent back, as a finder's fee. You know how, Erna. You learned all about finder's fees packaging mortgages, didn't you? After your divorce settlement, get ten percent of the taxes the IRS recovers from Michael Vevers—there is your one hundred thousand dollars."

"Edith, I might as well tell you that if Leroy Carlson buys, I get a three percent finder's fee. No one is hurt by that, are they?"

Edith put down the paper. "My God, how could you?"

"Leroy Carlson offered. Full disclosure. Of course I told Dad."

"Full of surprises, Erna, but then you always have been."

"Edith, please." I began to cry.

"Stop your damn crying. It's too late for crying."

"Please, Edith."

"Just quit your damn bawling."

Chapter 15

Erna

On the porch Dad has moved his table into the shade, to the right of the roof-supporting pillar. Dad sits facing the Gulf.

It was too early for the sunset beach walkers, too early for the after-work joggers. The gulls sit, their backs to the wind. Our resident crow complains from his palm tree. I place the tray on Dad's legal pad. Edith and Emmie sit themselves in the lounge chairs.

"Time for your orange juice break."

"I thought it was a delegation from Equal Rights for Women."

"'Equal Opportunity,' Dad."

"You got it. Equality for all, you have earned it."

"Dad, we had a meeting of minds."

"I am glad you all agreed. O.K., sit down."

"We have come to help you and Mama."

"Millie, Millie, come here. We have volunteers. Put them to work."

Mama came in from the kitchen. "Hurry up. I'm washing the broccoli."

"Sit down, Mama, have some orange juice. With calcium, fight osteoporosis."

"Thanks, Erna."

"We have decided you do less, we do more."

"I am ready."

"Dad, if there is anything I can do."

"Get started in Paris. I'll make you my agent for all of Europe, from Munich to Zurich."

"I am serious."

"I am, too. You could sell our prints in Europe. The Deutschmark is up, the British pound is up. We keep the sale proceeds in Europe, out of the reach of the tax collectors."

"Is that legal?"

"Depends on how it's done."

"Dad, isn't there something I could do now? This year."

"You want two lawsuits, IRS reviews. You want to spend your life fighting to prove you didn't do anything wrong? You want to manage a half-empty office building?"

"That's not all bad."

"It's not for kids."

"We are not kids."

"It's in Rock City, Erna. You forgot we have only one French restaurant. You wouldn't like the food there. Where would you get your Jaguar serviced?"

"In Davenport. There is a dealer in Davenport."

"O.K., the first one to come back to Rock City becomes the CEO of Kramer Companies."

"Tell them, Robert. No sense waiting."

"The good news: One lawsuit has been settled. The buyers will honor their note obligation. So, by 1999, instead of holding notes we will be paid out."

"That took, Dad, three and half years of litigation."

"More good news. We have begun to divide the properties. In ten years Edith and Frank get the office building under a grantor trust. That's the good news. If

Mom and I don't live ten more years, trust is void. We wasted the effort."

"Tell them, Robert."

"The lots are going up for sale, should sell too in cooperation with the city's effort to encourage low-cost housing. Our lots are the cheapest on the market."

"They shouldn't be if you are going to recover the cost of holding them for eleven years."

"Profit isn't everything, Erna."

"How much are you going to lose?"

"Not any more than I have to. Now for the best news. We planted twelve hundred assorted hardwoods, oak, and walnut. In forty years, you three will be the owners of western Illinois' most valuable tree farm. If we continue to reforest at the same rate, in three years we'll have the farm fully reforested."

"How much did that cost you, Dad?"

"Ask Edith. You can't take out without putting back. I'm spending the money we got for the cut timber on seedlings."

"How much are you out of pocket on the land on the taxes."

"I don't count. Can't put a dollar sign on reforestation."

"The IRS will when it comes to collecting estate taxes."

Dad laughs. "Our trust officer ran an actuarial projection on Mama and my longevity. We should be with you for exactly twenty years and six months from last May."

"Dad, I don't want hassles with the IRS over timber values. I don't know anything about timber."

"All taken care of. Ask the State Forester. He'll get you a low valuation—half grown trees aren't worth much. In fifty years when the trees are ready for cutting, you'll be rich as Rockefeller. Four thousand trees for three daughters."

"Dad, I am serious. I don't want hassles with the IRS over timber."

"As it says in Ecclesiastes, Erna, ain't no life or death for free. Them that has pays for them that don't. You has, you pays."

"Papa in fifty years we will all be dead."

"That's enough, Erna. You know how Papa feels about the farm."

"I know three thousand, or is it four thousand a year in taxes . . . That's sixty, seventy thousand dollars plus the cost of land. Dad, you have lost one hundred thousand dollars."

"Erna, don't talk to your father that way."

"O.K., in fifty years our grandchildren will own the farm."

As soon as Dad says that, Mama is there, calling, "Emmie, come on, help me. I have some herring and crackers."

Dad and Edith stay seated, which surprises me, because Edith . . . Well, Edith doesn't like it when we talk about grandchildren.

I say, "I am sorry, Dad."

Dad doesn't answer.

"I didn't mean to hurt you."

"I know, Erna, I know. Do you ever hear what you are saying to me? Mama would be pleased if I sold the farm. She doesn't like me tramping around those hills. She thinks I'll slip and fall into Kyte Creek, drown in four inches of water. Mama doesn't talk about money. Erna, try not talking about money."

"It's only for your own good."

"Now that is finished. We don't need an after-dinner meeting."

"Dad, you promised Carlson you would call him tomorrow."

"I will, or you can, Erna."

"What shall I tell him?"

"No sale. Two words. Not yet, not this year, not next year. Not any time soon will I sell the cottages."

"Why, Dad?"

"Mama doesn't want to live in a condo. She isn't ready for that. Mama doesn't like to be so far from the beach. Three floors up she can't hear the children playing. Anyway, three floors up is too far from the honeysuckle."

"What about my hundred thousand?"

"You get your hundred thousand. Tell us when you need it. Emmie gets hers, and you, Edith, you get hundred thousand. No quarrels until after your dad is dead."

"Thanks, Dad." I put my arms around Dad and kissed his forehead.

"Once a year I get a kiss from my daughter."

I didn't answer. I should have said, "I didn't kiss you because of the money you gave me," but I didn't. I couldn't.

Tomorrow I will tell Dad, "Thank you. That kiss was for caring, not for money." I don't really know why I don't kiss Dad. That is, I do know and I don't know.

"Mrs. Vevers, you must get over your fear of being abandoned. Your dad did not abandon you. He was in the army doing what he had to do. Go, forgive your dad, put your arms around him, tell him just once before he dies, 'Dad I love you.'"

Not yet. I am gaining on it. Dad, getting rid of Michael is the first step. Learning to live alone is next.

"Erna, forgiving your dad, why is that so hard for you?"

I don't know, Doctor. I don't know.

"Is it possible that you transferred your resentments from your father to Michael?"

"No, I don't think so. Michael beat me. My father never did."

"Neglect is abuse, too. Your dad didn't neglect you."

"He could have made up for it when he came home, but he was always too busy for me. Edith didn't need Dad, not so much as I did. For four years Edith had Dad all for herself. Emmie had Mama."

"Mrs. Vevers, I am delighted with your progress."

"So am I, Doctor."

Dad, I have been having some problems. One day I'll tell you all about them. That is, I'll write to you about my life. It's sort of complex. Dad, I do love you, but I didn't love you, not when I was little.

That's a long time ago, Erna.

I am sorry, Dad, one day I'll be able to kiss you. I'll come and put my arms around you, say, "Dad, I love you, forgive me."

"It's not your fault, Erna. We don't all respond to life with the same way. I saw that in the prison camp."

There he goes again, talking about himself.

"Erna, you want some herring?"

"Yes, Mama, thank you."

"Emmie, get Papa some *matza*. Papa likes *matza* with his herring."

"I know, Mama, I know."

Emmie serves, Edith clears, and I take in Papa's "writings" from the porch, his legal pads, the pillow he sits on. The pillow goes behind the loveseat in the living room. Papa's manuscripts go on the second shelf of the rattan secretary.

"What are you writing, Papa?"

Papa laughs. "I write what no one reads."

"I would read yours and Mama's biography."

"It's the third generation that is supposed to care about their grandparents."

"Not that again. You know Michael didn't want children. Don't say it, Papa. Don't say you could have left Michael, remarried, had children. Papa, I can't change what was."

"I know that." Papa laughed. "I can't very often change what is."

"One thing you can do for me, Papa."

"What, Erna?"

"Not only for be, but for Emmie and Edith. Tell us how it is for you. How it was for you."

"Why, Erna?"

"So I can understand where I come from."

"*Kuk nisht fun vannent die fis vaxen.*"

"What did you say?"

"Don't look from where your feet grow."

Chapter 16

Erna

I had truly thought that Papa would never tell. What surprised me was that Papa told as much as he did. It must be easier for Papa to write on his legal pads than to sit down to talk like a family. It's that—his fear of loss, fear of losing his daughters. Papa, father's don't lose daughters. Daughters lose fathers. Daughters fear that, Papa. Speak to Edith, she'll tell you, "I didn't want to be head of household." Ask Edith about the price she paid to help with Mama's estate. To be there in Chicago with the accountants, the attorneys dividing Mama's jewelry. Now Edith is Mama. What am I, Papa? That's what I thought I would learn from your letter journal writings. I found no answer. Nothing. What happened in the prison camp, Papa?

Papa, tell us how your life is without Mama. Tell me, Papa, did you love Mama?

The yellow pages arrived in Paris on April 21, dated the first week of Passover, our second Seder without Mama.

San Francisco
1992

My dear Erna,

You asked for a biography. What I have produced is somewhat less. It is for you to judge the extent of my "truth," which is limited by my selective memory and then its distortions to please myself. Perhaps it would have been better that I never ever written these few pages. Because now you, Erna, must decide whether and when you should share these with your sisters.

I was flattered that you were interested enough in your papa to be so insistent that I share my "head" with you. I do not expect that anything you read here will change the rest of your life. I remember when I was in the Army, receiving letters from my father, I said to myself I will be as he wants me to be, as he wishes me to be. I tried quite diligently, but I ended up as you see me, as I was to be. I became what I could bear. Like a dray horse whose harness falls into place, fitting where it is comfortable. From time to time I developed weeping, running pressure sores, all hidden by the harness. I could smell the necrotic, but it wasn't visible.

I don't want for you to worry – your father is not going to become a depressive. Not at my age. I am much too clever to seek ill health. As a way to gain a daughter's attentive care, I have taught myself to be cheerful and to look forward. Yes to December, January and February in Sanibel. I will stay longer, until Passover, no doubt. I know how busy you are in Paris.

Come to Sanibel if you can. You are always welcome. I am always pleased to see you. I have vowed to listen, to let you tell as much as you wish *with or without my additions, editorials, corrections. Who says your father is not aware of his deficiencies? At any rate, my intentions are there; whether I succeed is to be determined. Maybe I too can change. Ours is a world that changes. Each year in Sanibel the beach debris is unique. One year there are pen shell with opalescent linings and barnacle-encrusted bodies that crackle into reflective shards when I step on them. The next year there are the spring purple sea urchins. Another year it's the sand dollars that are everywhere. But always the coquinas are there for the sea birds to feed on. With change there is still the constant continuum, the sameness. The beach grass advances but only as far as the tide and the surf will tolerate. Toleration, balance, space — sounds like human behavior, doesn't it, Erna? I believe my head is still good. If I disturb you, you may attribute my misanthropy to the loss of your mother, to my unresolved problems with this and that. Any excuse you wish to defend your father.*

Surely you judge your father by his deeds of forty years than by this journal of some few pages.

You remember the last time we were all together with mama on Sanibel. When you so wanted the cottages sold? It was I who decided not to sell. I see your why. With all your arguments and plans for the sale, the why is simple. I heard a song: I want it all and I want it now. Just a chance that I had on MTV and not the CNN war. So, I said, "No," and it did not matter to you. The distribution of the dollars from Mama's estate has stopped all our talks about money. I said "No," and you got the money. Such is life. Plan, plan, and then failure or success we can't influence. You cannot indict Mama and me for any decision we reached in your behalf. I am too arrogant to care. I did what I thought best. Best at that time.

That's that. No more about dollars or francs or pesetas. Please, no more. Write to me about art and love and your hopes. You must bear the price for how often have you said, "Papa, how are you feeling? Papa, are you lonely? Papa, are you afraid of dying? Papa, I love you." You say all that and more to yourself. But say it out loud just once so you can hear it too. Like the confessional we recite together aloud on Yom Kippur. I write that because it's now too late for you to tell to your mother. I can hear you: "Don't lay the guilt on me, Papa." If there is guilt, the guilt is yours, Erna. No one, not even your father, can lay it on you. Mama and I never used money as a weapon. We should have. You would have saved a few years, but we were "modern" parents, respectful of our daughter's rights.

Don't answer this letter with "Dear Father, You made it too easy to take. You asked too little of me, Papa. Now, Papa, you want your guilt payment."

No, I want you to know I no longer have the time to do all the things I was going to do gently, explain to you quietly while we walked to the lighthouse. Erna, you are of our flesh. We love you. We hurt when you hurt. Forgive me for my sins of commission, for my sins of omission, for my arrogance, for my prejudices, for that which you dislike in me and that you have kindness enough never to tell me. We were to sit face to face, the sun already set, the lights on in the cottage. Your mother has lit the Sabbath candles. We are late for dinner. You were to kiss me and say, "You didn't have to say all that, Papa. I love you, Papa."

You watch me pray and once you asked me, "What did God do for you?" God is civilization, deeds of loving kindness, protection for the widows, the poor, the orphan. For me, personally, God comes and gives.

Mama and I gave up instructing you when you were about eighteen or seventeen, when you went off to State. I can't remember but I am sure when we left you at the dorm, we put our arms around you and kissed you. Why? When was it that our hugs and kisses became intolerable to you? There is no need to discuss the past. The future is yours. Do as you wish. We will always love you.

Yours,
R.K.

P.S. There are, I believe, six letters that through the years your mother wrote to you but never mailed. I gave them to Edith. You may ask for them, if you wish. The letters complain of your language usage. The others are pleas for more love than you were able to give. Your mother did not whine or protest about her daughters, not even to me. Your mother felt she deserved more love, companionship, sharing, little days alone with you. For me, I learned a long time ago to be satisfied with my portion. It is strange what upset your mother most. All those years we visited with you in San Francisco, never once did you introduce her to your friends. I always told her, "Erna just wants to spend the time with you alone."
R.K.

Made in the USA
Charleston, SC
10 June 2014